"I want you."

Chase shuddered from the pleasure that Sunny's words brought him. Should he have known how much he wanted to hear them?

"This is crazy," he said and was surprised at the husky sound of his voice.

"Yes." Sunny smiled as she tugged his tie loose and then dropped it on the floor of the limo.

"We can't," he protested, but the tantalizing scrape of her nails against his skin as she undid his buttons kept him from stopping her.

"We can," she murmured as she nibbled at his lower lip. "And we will. No one can interrupt us here."

"Except the driver." But even as he said the words, he was pulling down the thin straps of her dress.

"But you're so efficient. I'm sure you told him to just keep on driving."

And of course, he had.

Carolyn Andrews would love to have a professional shopper like Sunny Caldwell in her life. As Carolyn explains it: "My fantasies have always been fairly simple. And the idea of never again having to battle my way through the crowded aisles of a grocery store ranks pretty high on my wish list."

Books by Carolyn Andrews

HARLEQUIN TEMPTATION
498—CJ'S DEFENSE

SERVICE WITH A SMILE

CAROLYN ANDREWS

Harlequin Books

TORONTO • NEW YORK • LONDON
AMSTERDAM • PARIS • SYDNEY • HAMBURG
STOCKHOLM • ATHENS • TOKYO • MILAN
MADRID • WARSAW • BUDAPEST • AUCKLAND

To my dad and my brother,
the two Andrews in my life.

Special thanks to my godchild, Emma,
and to Sara, Nicholas, Ryan and Conor
for helping me create Jason and Emma.

ISBN 0-373-25628-0

SERVICE WITH A SMILE

Copyright © 1995 by Carolyn Hanlon.

Printed in U.S.A.

1

SUNNY CALDWELL stepped through the door fully prepared to storm the lion's den. But one glance around the foyer of the Plum Court apartment building had her changing her metaphor. Wide-eyed, she crossed the marble-floored walkway to a bank of elevators. Miniature lights twinkled from the potted trees on either side of the narrow bridge. Overhead, a crystal chandelier caught the first rays of the morning sun and sent prisms of light dancing everywhere.

Delighted, Sunny turned in a full circle to take it all in. No, Chase Monroe did not live in a lion's den. He lived in a palace.

In the penthouse. A prince trapped in a tower? Even as the image formed in her mind, she pushed it aside. Wrong metaphor again, she scolded herself as she stepped into the elevator and pressed the button for the top floor. Chase Monroe III was not a prince. He was a retired news correspondent turned writer. And she certainly wasn't here to rescue him. Reporters, retired or not, were not among her favorite people. She wouldn't be here at all if her aunt Marnie hadn't bullied her into mailing him a brochure and if his secretary hadn't called to set up an appointment. Now she couldn't afford to pass up the opportunity of making this sale. And if she wanted a fairy-tale ending for her presentation today, she'd better concentrate on business.

As Sunny watched the floor numbers light up in slow progression, she focused on strategy. The success of any service business depended on meeting the customer's needs. For most of her clients, she stressed money. She could save them up to twenty percent of what they spent on groceries every week. But Chase Monroe came from money. Enough to buy himself half ownership in a local TV station and enough to get himself regularly written up in the society columns since his arrival in Syracuse six months ago.

The elevator doors slid open, and Sunny stepped onto the plush carpet that formed a narrow path to the door at the end of the hallway. No, money wasn't the key to selling Chase on Service with a Smile. A wealthy bachelor could probably get his grocery shopping done for free. It was only working mothers and the elderly who looked upon her as their savior. With Chase Monroe, she was going to emphasize the time-saving potential of using Service with a Smile. A man who was trying to juggle running a TV station and writing a book should appreciate that.

Her first two knocks brought no response. She'd raised her hand a third time when she saw the knob turn. A second later, it moved again.

When the door swung open, she found herself facing a little boy with huge brown eyes. Quickly she checked the number on the door. Had she copied it down wrong?

"You don't look anything like a grandmother," the boy said.

"Thank goodness for that." Sunny grinned as she glanced down at him. He couldn't be more than six or seven, and he was wearing striped pajamas.

"I'm looking for Chase Monroe," she said.

"Uncle Chase is in the shower. Are you going to be our nanny?"

"No, I—"

"Jason."

Sunny looked up to see Chase Monroe at the end of the hall. He wore nothing but a towel that rode low on his hips. She couldn't take her eyes off it as he strode toward them. She wanted to turn and run. But her feet wouldn't obey. Finally she managed to move her gaze from the knot in the towel up the path of curly hair to his broad shoulders, still wet from his shower. His skin seemed smooth and slick. She could almost imagine how it would feel under her hands. The coolness of the water, the warmth beneath.

When he squatted down in front of her to talk to the boy, the towel parted, revealing the entire length of one firmly muscled thigh.

Sunny tried to shift her gaze to the floor. Then she tried for the ceiling. But she finally found herself focusing on his tan line. It was very distinct. When was the last time she'd had nothing more important to do than lie in the sun and work on a tan? Had she ever been that carefree? This winter, she promised herself. She'd collect all the money on her past-due accounts and fly to a Caribbean island to work on developing tan lines.

"Jason, I don't want you to open the door to anybody. Understand?"

"You were in the shower," the boy replied, and then inserted his thumb into his mouth.

"I know." Chase patted the boy's shoulder. "Next time come and get me. Now can you do me a big favor and go check on your sister?"

Swallowing, Sunny wrenched her attention from Chase's tan line to his face. The strong chin and angled cheekbones were familiar to her from his television campaign to save the symphony. But with his hair damp and tousled from the shower, he looked different, less civilized. Was that why her stomach was twisting in knots?

"You're early."

It was an accusation. Sunny blinked and snapped out of her trance. "I'm right on time."

"I told the agency to send you at nine o'clock. It's barely seven." He glanced at his wrist and found it bare.

With great satisfaction, Sunny thrust her own watch under his nose. "It's eight o'clock. That's exactly when your secretary said to come."

His gaze swept over her, taking in the jeans, the denim shirt and the tan linen blazer. From her shoulder hung a purse that might have room for a wallet and car keys, but not much else. And she carried a briefcase. A briefcase? Chase's eyes narrowed as he studied her more closely. She didn't look like his idea of a nanny. She was too small, too delicate. And her hair was red. Not strawberry blond or auburn. It was the color of flames leaping hot and bright from a campfire. He could almost feel the heat. One unruly curl had escaped from a ribbon to fall along her cheek. Without thinking, he reached out to tuck it behind her ear.

Startled by his action, Chase dropped his hand to his side. He didn't make a habit of touching women casually. Especially strangers. Later, he would recall how soft her skin felt, how silky her hair. Right now, he frowned. "You're not what I expected."

Ditto, she thought as she drew in a shaky breath. Nerves. That was what had made her skin tingle at the brief contact. Just nerves. Praying her voice would work, she said, "I have it on good authority I don't look like a grandmother."

"Uncle Chase, Emma unplugged your clock."

They both shifted their attention to the two children walking toward them. The little girl was about five, Sunny guessed, and she had the same dark brown hair the little boy had, but hers fell in tangled curls almost to her waist.

"Well, that's one mystery solved," Chase said as he turned back to Sunny. "And I'll bet you're not Mrs. Winthrop, the nanny from the Hudson Agency."

"No. I'm Sunny Caldwell from Service with a Smile. I mailed you a brochure a few weeks ago, and your secretary set up this appointment."

His eyes narrowed fractionally in recognition. Then he smiled. Sunny was sure she felt the warmth spread right down to her toes.

"I'm sorry," he said. "I . . . Things have been hectic since the . . . kids arrived." He glanced down, suddenly aware of his lack of clothes. When he met her eyes this time, she could see a trace of amusement. "Won't you come in? Make yourself at home while I slip into something more . . . comfortable."

As he walked past the children, the little girl grabbed the towel. It fell to the floor with the finality of a third-act curtain.

Without breaking stride, Chase scooped the child up in his arms and continued on down the hall.

Sunny stared at his disappearing derriere, trying to convince herself what she'd just seen hadn't happened. But the towel lay on the floor where it had fallen. One long wolf whistle was what the situation called for. But she couldn't even pucker her lips.

Jason tugged at her hand and asked in a whisper, "Did you see his bare butt?"

"Yes, I certainly did."

The little boy glanced up and gave her a tentative smile.

"Uncle Chase is funny, isn't he?"

Sunny smiled back at him. "He sure is."

"I'm hungry." Jason led the way down the hall and through an archway into the kitchen.

It was a perfectly square room with a wide counter dividing it in two. Jason made a beeline for the refrigerator and took out a carton of milk and a colorful cereal box.

"Your uncle keeps cereal in the refrigerator?" Sunny asked, setting her briefcase on the counter. When she walked over to shut the door, she saw that the shelves were bare.

"No. I put it in there to keep the milk company. Can I have a bowl?"

Most of the cupboards were empty, too, Sunny discovered as she located two bowls and spoons. Then she watched in horror as Jason poured the milk. The instant it hit the cereal, it turned blue.

"What is that?"

"Bluegaloos," Jason mumbled around his first mouthful. After swallowing, he continued, "On our way from the airport last night, Uncle Chase let me pick out whatever I wanted." He scooped up another mouthful. "Do you cook?"

"Some. Why?"

"Emma won't eat this."

Smart girl, Sunny thought. "Didn't she tell your uncle what she wanted?"

Jason shook his head. "She doesn't talk anymore. Not since Mommy and Daddy went away. They went up in a plane, and it crashed. Uncle Chase says we'll be living with him now." This time the spoon wavered on the way to his mouth.

Sunny's heart twisted, but she was saved from replying when Emma appeared in the archway. Crossing to her, Sunny held out her hand. "Let's find something for you to eat." The little girl followed her to the double-doored cupboard that seemed the most likely place for groceries. It was empty except for a bottle of champagne, a jar of imported caviar and a box of English water biscuits.

"Just the essentials," Sunny murmured giddily. Kneeling down, she delivered the bad news to Emma. "Do you know the nursery rhyme about Old Mother Hubbard?"

The little girl stared at her solemnly. Sunny had to fight against the urge to smooth the tangles out of her hair. "Uncle Chase's cupboards are almost as empty. Want to check it out?" There was still no reply, but when she held out her arms, Emma walked into them. Lifting her easily, Sunny pointed to the champagne. "You're too young for the bubbly, but I suppose it's never too early for a girl to develop a taste for caviar. Are you game?"

She was reaching for the jar when Emma pointed over her shoulder. Turning, Sunny found herself looking at a reproduction of Georgia O'Keefe's *Yellow Cactus Flowers.* It was attached to a calendar hanging by the phone. Odd that a man like Chase Monroe would choose Georgia O'Keefe. Granted, the picture was beautiful, but somehow she would have expected something else. Like what? Playmate of the Year?

Almost automatically, she dropped her gaze to the square containing the day's date. Written in a very masculine hand were the words "Interview Leo Caldwell's niece—8:00 a.m." Stunned, she blinked and read it again.

Closing her eyes, she struggled against the surge of temper. Why should it surprise her that Chase Monroe might have his own agenda for agreeing to meet with her? After all, he'd spent most of his life in the newsgathering business. And as a recently jailed state senator, Leo Caldwell was still news.

Opening her eyes, she read the notation on the calendar again: "Interview Leo Caldwell's niece." Everything made sense now. Use the niece to get to the uncle. It had worked a year ago for a reporter who worked at Chase's TV station. Jeff Miller had made quite a name for himself with the series of interviews he'd done with Leo Caldwell. Why shouldn't it work again?

Sunny took two deep breaths and forced herself to think. Just because Chase Monroe had his own agenda it didn't have to affect her own. She was here to sell him on Service with a Smile. That was her primary goal. Not only did she need his business, she reminded herself, but she also needed his help to gain entry into the social circles he traveled in. And no one was going to use her again to get to Uncle Leo.

A tug on her hair brought her attention back to the little girl she was holding. "So you like my hair ribbon, do you?" She carried Emma to a stool. "How about if we put it in *your* hair?"

"She usually wears a braid," Jason said. "Our mommy said it keeps the tangles out. Emma cries when she gets tangles."

"I don't blame her." Sunny fished a small hairbrush out of her purse. "Isn't it lucky I'm an expert on braiding? When I was a little girl, my father brushed my hair every night, and he never made me cry." While she spoke, she drew the brush gently through Emma's hair.

CHASE STEPPED into his loafers and pulled a sweater over his head. His appointment with Sunny Caldwell had completely slipped his mind. But then, he hadn't been able to keep his mind on much of anything since David and Laura's plane crash.

It still didn't seem real. None of it. How could it be that only one week ago, he'd stood with Emma and Jason waving to his brother and sister-in-law as their small plane whipped past them on the runway and rose slowly into the air?

Everything since that moment seemed like a dream. The news of the crash, the funeral, the details of the will. The trip back with the children. And now. Turning, he let his gaze sweep the room. This was real. Jason and Emma were his responsibility now. Glancing down, he spotted his wallet and retrieved it from the bedside table.

Miss Caldwell and her notorious uncle would have to wait until he managed to fit his niece and nephew into his life.

Jason's giggle drew him to the kitchen. He hadn't heard the little boy laugh since the accident. In the archway Chase paused to take in the scene. His nephew sat cross-legged on the counter directing the styling of his sister's hair.

"No. It starts higher. On the top of her head."

"Oh, a French braid." Sunny nodded, starting over. "Those are trickier to do. Like this?"

"Sort of," Jason replied, getting up on his knees to take a closer look. "Yeah."

Chase remained where he was. During the six months he'd lived in the apartment, he'd seldom used the kitchen. It had always seemed so sterile. Now with sunlight streaming through the windows and the laughter of a child, it seemed warm, welcoming.

Fascinated, he watched Sunny draw the strands of Emma's hair through her slender fingers. Her hands were small like the rest of her, the nails short and unpainted. As they moved quickly and skillfully through his niece's hair, he wondered how they might feel on his skin.

With a frown he glanced at Sunny's face. First, he'd touched her. Now he wanted to know what it might feel like if she touched him. What was it about her? Leaning against the wall, he studied her. She had a small compact body, most of which seemed to be legs. And that hair. Freed from its ribbon, it fell in a tumble of curls to just brush her shoulders. The sun only heightened the fiery color.

As Sunny tied the ribbon on Emma's braid, she felt his eyes on her. Glancing over, she felt a tingle of awareness race through her. The black turtleneck sweater and jeans covered almost every inch of him, but they did very little to disguise what lay underneath.

She forced her eyes upward and found that the lines of his face were as chiseled and hard as the rest of him. The quiet intensity of his gaze offered a challenge that had her chin lifting. When she'd come through the front door, she'd thought of him as a lion. How appropriate, she thought now. Lean, powerful . . . a predator. Admiration and apprehension moved through her.

"I owe you an apology," he said.

"For what?" she asked. Then a mischievous light flashed in her eyes. "I didn't see anything you have to apologize for."

"I didn't mean . . ." He felt the sudden rush of blood to his cheeks. Good Lord, was he blushing?

Sunny laughed. A rich, vibrant sound. "I'm sorry, but I couldn't resist." Feeling Emma's tug on her sleeve, she lifted the little girl off the stool, then returned her gaze to Chase. "So, what's the apology for?"

"I told my secretary to clear my schedule for the rest of the week. She must have overlooked you because we were meeting here, instead of at the office. Why don't you call her next week and we'll reschedule?"

"Why?"

"I beg your pardon?"

"Why reschedule? I'm here now. I can explain the shopping services I provide. You could definitely use some groceries. Jason says Emma won't eat that blue goop, and I don't think her palate is sophisticated enough for caviar." Shifting Emma to her hip, she flipped open her briefcase and removed some forms. "Let me show you." When she turned to spread them on the counter, she inadvertently bumped into him.

"Sorry." Even as she took a quick step away, she raised her eyes to meet his. Nerves again. She always had to deal with them when she made a presentation. But never had they made her so aware of another person. Even now she could feel the heat pulse through her from each and every point her body had connected with his. His eyes told her nothing. She couldn't even be sure of their color. Gray maybe, but with hints of green. All she could really see was the image of herself trapped in them.

Swallowing to ease the dryness in her throat, Sunny forced herself to look back at the forms. "They're very easy to fill out." She ran her finger across the even columns of an order blank. "Even if you're not a regular shopper." She risked a quick sideways glance. "You probably eat out a lot."

"I don't cook."

She nodded, shifting one of the forms to the top of the pile. "Well, with the children here, you'll need food in the house. Milk, orange juice, cereal, that sort of thing. This lists many of the ready-to-eat foods that are available in most markets. You can get pizza, salads, Italian specialties, even Chinese. Grocery stores are willing to do a lot to take the chore of cooking off your hands."

Hands. Chase suddenly realized he was staring at her hands again as her fingers skimmed quickly down the columns of a new form. She was rattling off information on brand names, sizes, categories of foods. He wouldn't have been able to repeat one thing if his life depended on it.

Chase moved to the other side of the counter and said, "I've hired a nanny. Part of her job will be to take care of all that. Mrs. Winthrop. She's due to arrive at nine o'clock."

Sunny met his gaze squarely. "Then you invited me here under false pretenses."

"What do you mean?"

"You never had any intention of purchasing my services. You just set up this appointment to see if you could dig up some more dirt on my uncle, didn't you? Well, it won't work."

"Ms. Caldwell, I—"

"Don't bother to lie. I've run into your type before."

For the second time in as many minutes, Chase felt the blood rushing to his face. Ridiculous. To be embarrassed by this pint-size urchin with a mop of red hair. Even worse, there was an element of truth to her accusation. He opened his mouth, but just then the phone rang, and he didn't have to attempt an explanation.

"Wait," he said as he left the kitchen and walked down the hall to pick up the extension in his den.

Sunny drew in a deep breath and counted to ten. She was going to leave without losing her temper. Chase Monroe might have a great body and a heart-melting smile, but he was as small-minded and mean as the other members of the press, who had swarmed around her uncle after his indictment. And if it came to a choice between increasing her profit margins and protecting her uncle, well, there was no choice. Still holding Emma on her hip, she began to toss order blanks back into her briefcase.

"Are you mad at Uncle Chase?" Jason asked. He was sitting on the counter, his hands gripping the edge.

Sunny's anger melted the moment she met the little boy's eyes. "No." Instinctively she tightened her hold on Emma. Despite what she thought of Chase Monroe personally, she could only imagine what he'd been going through in the past few days. "We just had a little misunderstanding. Nothing important."

Chase reappeared in the archway. "I have to leave."

"Fine." She walked toward him. "I'll help you get the children ready."

"They can't come. There's an emergency at the station." He glanced at his watch. "I'm sorry. There's no time to explain. Can you stay until Mrs. Winthrop arrives? She'll be here in half an hour."

"Now wait just a minute." Sunny held Emma out to him, but he merely dropped a kiss on her forehead, then stepped to the counter to pat Jason on the shoulder. "Take care of your sister, and do what Mrs. Winthrop says."

"Hey. . ." Sunny hurried after him as he strode down the hall. "If you think you can—" She reached the door just as he closed it firmly in her face. "Damn!"

"That's a bad word," Jason said.

She glanced down at him and once more felt her anger disappear. The little boy had such a solemn expression on his face. "Yeah. I used to get my mouth washed out with soap a lot."

"Soap?" His eyes widened. "Ugh."

"Nah. I loved it! I could blow these huge bubbles. Want to try some?"

Jason grinned. "No way."

"C'mon." She shifted Emma to a more comfortable position on her hip and took Jason's hand. "Show me where your clothes are. You better get dressed before Mrs. Winthrop arrives."

They'd taken only two steps before Jason tugged her to a stop. "Is Uncle Chase going to come back?"

Sunny squeezed his hand. "Definitely. He hasn't had a chance to taste those Bluegaloos yet. How could he pass up a treat like that?"

AN HOUR AND A HALF later, Sunny stood on the back porch of The Growing Place, Heather Kelly's day-care center. The yard was filled with the sound of shouts and laughter. When they'd first arrived, the children had clung to her for a short time. But eventually Jason had wandered off to watch the older kids on the jungle gym. And Heather's daughter, Amanda, had coaxed Emma away to play in the sandbox.

"Let me get this straight." Heather shifted the infant she was holding to her shoulder. "You fired their nanny?"

"You should have seen her." Sunny paced back and forth. "The second she walked in the door, she told me I shouldn't be holding Emma. She didn't believe in coddling children. *Coddling!*" Still furious, Sunny paused at the porch railing and looked out over the sun-splashed lawn. Four of Heather's staff members were supervising playtime. Each of them held a child. "I told her that I'd never heard of coddled children, only coddled eggs."

Heather grinned. "I'll bet she warmed right up to you then."

Sunny watched her friend settle the baby in the crook of her arm. With her long blond hair pulled into a ponytail, Heather didn't look much older than the kids she cared for. "That woman was so stiff and cold I'll bet she had starch in her underwear."

Heather's expression was serious when she met Sunny's eyes. "Still, it wasn't your place to fire her."

Sunny's chin lifted. "Their uncle deserted them. Left them with me, a stranger, with barely so much as a by-your-leave."

"He did mention an emergency."

"Hmph. I have a few things to say to Chase Monroe."

"What's he like? Is he as handsome as he is on television?"

Chase's image flashed into Sunny's mind. She could clearly picture the tousled hair, still damp from the shower, the slanted cheekbones, the strong chin. And that long, lean body wearing nothing but a towel. She felt the heat flood her face.

Heather's delighted laugh filled the air. "I don't believe it. You're blushing. What happened?"

Sunny frowned as her color deepened even further. "Nothing. He could probably accuse me of kidnapping his niece and nephew. Does that sound like the start of a big romance? And besides, he's a reporter. I know better than to get mixed up with one of them. Don't look at me like that. You're as bad as Aunt Marnie. She was the one who badgered me into sending him the brochure in the first place. Why did I ever listen to her?"

"Because you need to expand your customer base to include a richer clientele. Isn't that what you've been saying for the past year? Your aunt was only trying to help."

Sunny waved a hand. "Yeah. But she has her own agenda."

Heather tilted her head to the side as she continued to study Sunny. "This time I think your aunt Marnie may be onto something."

"Mommy!" Sunny glanced down to see Amanda climbing the porch steps with Emma in tow. "She has to go to the bathroom."

"Did she tell you that?" asked Sunny.

Amanda shook her head as she led Emma into the house.

"She's making her needs known even if she isn't speaking," Heather said. "That's a good sign."

Sunny glanced over to where Jason was sitting on one of the lower bars on the jungle gym. She smiled and waved at him. "Jason worries me, too. He seems to be handling things on the surface, but he's too quiet. Or maybe cautious is a better word. As if he's afraid he'll do something wrong."

"They've suffered a terrible loss. It will take time for them to heal," Heather said. "Time and love."

"Could you take them here on a permanent basis? I know you have a waiting list."

"For you, I'll always have room. I wouldn't have this place if you hadn't persuaded your uncle Leo to rent it to me. But it's their uncle who has to make that decision."

"This has got to be better for them than sitting in an apartment with Mary Poppins from hell. Surely he'll be able to see that."

"Day care isn't as convenient as live-in help," Heather cautioned.

The clanging of a bell started a stampede of children up the steps.

"Snack time," Heather explained.

"Talk about Pavlov's dog." Sunny shook her head as she watched the yard clear in a matter of seconds. "I have to check in at my office. I told the kids I'd be gone about an hour."

"Take your time. They'll be fine."

Leaving her car in Heather's driveway, Sunny cut across the playground of The Growing Place. A warm breeze carried the scent of roses. The carriage house that now served as her home and office sat on the far end of Uncle Leo's property and bordered her family's backyard.

For thirty years, the Caldwell brothers had lived back-to-back, but their two homes couldn't have been more different. Leo's house had once served as the headmaster's quarters of a private military academy. It boasted twenty-four rooms and sat on two acres of grass and trees. Sunny's father's home was part of the development that had been built when the school buildings had been leveled. The down payment had been a wedding gift from Leo to his younger brother.

When she was growing up, the carriage house had been her father's secret hideaway. A place where he could work on his inventions and dream his dreams. After his death, it had sat empty for ten years. Now she was using it to make her own dreams come true.

The muted thrumming of heavy-metal rock told her that her assistant, Hector Rodriguez, was hard at work at his computer. But any hope Sunny had of rushing into her office to save Hector from annihilating his eardrums was destroyed when her aunt Marnie hailed her from the back porch of her parents' house.

"Sunny!" Slightly plump, with a soft pretty face framed in fluffy gray curls, Marnie looked like everyone's favorite aunt. Sweet, gentle, harmless. About as harmless as a hurricane, Sunny reminded herself as she summoned up a smile and tried to ready herself for the inquisition.

"How did your meeting go with Mr. Monroe? No, don't answer until you wheel me inside. It's almost time for my show."

"Which one?" Sunny asked as she pushed the wheelchair through the open door and into the den.

"'As the River Runs.' Your aunt Alma and I have a bet that Slade is the man who killed Jared Mars. But it doesn't start until after the noon news. We have time to talk."

Once inside the room, Sunny let Marnie take control of her chair, watching her angle it so that she had a clear view of both the television set and the backyard. Born in a time before children with cerebral palsy attended regular schools, Marnie had led a rather sheltered life. Then her parents had died and left her in the care of her sister, Alma, and two brothers. Leo Caldwell had immediately installed Marnie and Alma in his home. After all, he explained, as a state senator, he had to spend most of his time in Albany, anyway. He said they were doing him a favor to live there and run the place for him. Sunny felt the sudden push of tears behind her eyes and blinked hard. Generous to a fault. That was the Uncle Leo she knew. In his care, his two sisters had blossomed. Especially Marnie.

"Here, taste this." Carrying a bowl, Alma strode into the room and thrust a spoon under Sunny's nose.

Sunny obediently swallowed what was offered.

"What d'ya think?" Alma demanded.

"More salt," Sunny replied.

Alma turned to glare at her sister. "I told you it needed more salt."

"Salt's bad for you," Marnie said to her sister's retreating back.

"Hogwash! You've been watching too many talk shows."

In response to Sunny's raised brows, Marnie sighed. "I think your aunt Alma is suffering from boredom."

"Boredom?" Sunny said. It was hard to imagine Aunt Alma being bored. At five-ten with the build of a linebacker, the woman seemed to be constantly in motion.

"This house is so much smaller than Leo's. Alma doesn't have enough to keep her busy, so she's thrown herself into a cooking frenzy! She has a regular test kitchen going out there." Marnie began to tap her fingers on the arm of her wheelchair. "She's driving me nuts. I'm going to have to find something for Alma to channel her energy into, besides our food. Or I might end up poisoned. But sit." Marnie beckoned Sunny closer. "Tell me what happened with Chase Monroe."

"Nothing happened." Sunny perched on the arm of a chair and highlighted the morning's events.

When she finished, Marnie said, "That's good. Better than I'd hoped for."

Sunny stared at her in astonishment. "Good? What if he has me arrested for kidnapping his niece and nephew?"

"Well, the children do add a slight complication. But he'll definitely need Service with a Smile now. I was so worried he was called away before you got to meet with him."

"How did you know he was called away?"

"It's been on television all morning." Marnie aimed the remote control at the TV set and pressed a button. "Some poor disturbed man in Pennville walked into the beauty salon his ex-wife runs in her home and pulled a gun on her and their two-year-old son."

As Marnie spoke, the logo for Channel 7 "News at Noon" faded to a shot of Chase Monroe on a sunny sidewalk in Pennville, New York. Behind him, a row of police cars served as a barricade holding back curious onlookers.

Chase spoke into his microphone. "The police have just confirmed that Matthew Anderson has agreed to let his wife and son leave the premises. They're coming out now." Sunny stared at the screen as the camera focused on a young woman walking out of a house, carrying a child.

"Chase is covering that story?" Sunny asked. She began to pace in the small room. "So he's decided to go back to reporting. Well, that certainly explains—"

"Oh, no. He's just filling in temporarily until they hire and train someone to replace Jeff Miller."

Sunny stopped in her tracks. "He's what?"

"It was in the paper last weekend. Aunt Alma and I didn't want to mention it to you. We thought it might upset you. Jeff Miller is leaving Syracuse for a big job with a Chicago news station."

"Well, that certainly tears it!"

"Oh, dear, you are upset. It's really for the best. After what that Miller man did to you, you still can't have feel—"

Sunny waved a hand. "This isn't about what Jeff Miller did to me. It's what he did to Uncle Leo. He twisted everything Uncle Leo said so that even Uncle Leo's most loyal supporters turned against him!"

"Sunny, none of that was your fault."

"No? Before those interviews aired, no one believed that Uncle Leo would go to jail."

She paused to point an accusing finger at Chase's image on the TV screen. "And he's doing the same thing. He only agreed to see me because he wants to get more dirt on Uncle Leo. I should never have let you talk me into mailing him that brochure."

"You don't have to worry about Chase. He's not at all like Jeff Miller. Chase reminds me of Rafe on 'Gallagher's Dream.'"

"This isn't a soap opera. And one reporter is just as bad as another."

"How can you say that?" Marnie smiled at the TV screen, "Chase Monroe has the kind of face you can trust."

Oh, yes, thought Sunny as she studied his image and frowned. It was the kind of face designed to win a woman's trust. Those eyes—even on TV, she could feel their intensity. But they belonged to a reporter. She turned to Marnie. "Well, I don't trust him. He never had any intention of using Service with a Smile. He only scheduled the appointment with me to pump me about Uncle Leo."

"Oh? Did he tell you that?"

"He had me written in on his calendar as Leo Caldwell's niece. What does that tell you? Oh, I've learned my lesson about believing anyone involved with the press."

Marnie met Sunny's eyes steadily. "Can you afford to let your prejudice against reporters stand in the way of your business? You still need Chase Monroe as a client. And he certainly needs you."

Sunny sighed. "Yeah, but it's going to be difficult to convince him of that. First I have to sell him on taking the children to Heather, instead of rehiring that nanny." She glanced at her watch. "I have to go. I promised Emma and Jason I'd be back in an hour, and Hector awaits me."

Marnie didn't smile until Sunny had hurried out of the room. Things were working out even better than she'd hoped.

2

WHEN CHASE FIRST SAW HER sleeping on his couch, he blinked and took another look. Sunny Caldwell had slipped into his mind often that day. Was it happening again?

No, she was real, he decided as he stepped into the room. Emma was cradled in Sunny's arm, and Jason was fast asleep, sucking his thumb, his head pillowed on her lap. One of the secretaries at the station had mentioned that Sunny had called twice to say that the children were fine. Odd, but he hadn't worried for a minute after he'd left them with her.

Cocooned in the flickering light from the silent television set, they looked peaceful. Almost like a family. He moved closer. David and Laura's children. He felt the love well up in him.

Pausing just outside the circle of light, he switched his gaze to Sunny and studied her for a moment. She was the last person he'd expected to see tonight. And yet it wasn't only surprise he was feeling. Even now, asleep, there was something about her. Something that pulled at him.

She certainly wasn't beautiful, not in any classic sense. Her nose turned up at the end. Her mouth was a bit too wide, her chin too pointed.

Still, there was a softness about her. A fragility. He looked at the hand that lay protectively across Emma's arm. So delicate, and yet there was a strength there, too. Was it the contrast he found so intriguing? And her hair. It looked darker tumbled across her cheek, more auburn. He lifted a curl and rubbed it between his fingers. It felt impossibly soft and cool. Earlier, it had reminded him of fire, full of heat and sparks. Even in the dim light, he saw that each strand was a different shade of red or gold. Her scent drifted up to him, light and floral, as he tucked the curl gently behind her ear.

Sunny stirred the moment she felt his touch. Her eyes, dreamy, fogged with sleep, took only seconds to clear. "Oh. It's you." She glanced down at Emma. "They wanted to stay up until you came home."

"I'll take Jason." He lifted the boy easily into his arms. Sunny gathered up Emma and followed him down the hall to the bedroom. After tucking the little girl beneath the covers, she turned to watch Chase gently easing Jason's thumb out of his mouth. With a sigh, the little boy turned over and snuggled into his pillow.

"I wouldn't worry about him sucking his thumb." She spoke softly as she led the way into the kitchen.

"His mother used to worry about it when he was younger. I thought he stopped a few years ago."

Flipping on the light, Sunny moved to the other side of the wide counter that divided the room. "It's probably only temporary. I taught kindergarten for three years. You'd be amazed at how many of those little ones sucked their thumbs right through the month of September. The stress is unbelievable. But once they settled in, they usually quit." Propping her elbow on the counter, she held up her thumb. "It's a great stress buster and such a small thing to get comfort from. I can't see the harm. Eventually Jason will quit, too."

"Did he talk to you about what happened?" Chase asked.

"He mentioned the plane crash and that Emma had stopped speaking."

Chase sat down across from her. "Her pediatrician seems quite certain that she'll speak again soon. In the meantime, I'm not supposed to make a fuss about it, and when she does say something, I'm to carry on as usual."

Reaching across the counter, Sunny took one of his hands. It was clenched in a fist. She held it in both of hers.

After a moment, Chase continued, "David, my stepbrother, flies his own plane." He paused. "Flew. I always tried to join them on Cape Cod every summer. For at least a week. This year I could only go for the weekend. I took the kids fishing that day, and David took Laura up in the plane to give her a lesson. He'd been pushing her to get her pilot's license." He shrugged. "They're not even sure what caused the accident."

"I'm sorry." Even as she said the words, Sunny realized how inadequate they were. She tightened her hold on his hand and found that her fingers had become linked with his. His palms were rough, she realized, glancing down in surprise. Not what she'd expect from a writer. And they were large, his fingers long, the nails blunt and well shaped. Her own hand seemed completely lost in his. Seeing that only tightened the strange knot that had formed in her stomach.

She glanced up to find him looking at her with the same quiet intensity she'd noticed earlier. Immediately she released him.

She's nervous, Chase thought. He could see it in the way she clasped her hands together on the counter, then dropped them to her side. So she wasn't completely at ease around him. Slowly he smiled. "Do you think thumbs would work for adults?"

"Thumbs?"

"To relieve stress."

She managed an answering smile and saw for the first time how tired he looked. "I have to admit I tried it myself a few times, but it didn't seem to have the same effect that it does for the younger set."

"I've heard that adults have other, more pleasurable ways of dealing with stress."

The teasing light in his eyes left little doubt about his meaning. "Yes, well..." She lifted her chin when she felt the color staining her cheeks, then turned to the refrigerator. "Champagne is good." She took the bottle out along with the small jar of caviar. "Or so I've heard."

Chase grinned. "Sorry. I couldn't resist. I'm just getting even for this morning. You had me at a disadvantage."

She might have disagreed about which of them was at the greater disadvantage, but she didn't want to think about Chase Monroe wearing nothing but a towel. She'd thought about it often that day. Too often, in fact, she thought as she placed everything on the counter and then hurried to the cupboard.

Not that the image bothered her. Not at all. It was the feelings it triggered. Even now she could feel the sudden tightening in her stomach as if she was anticipating a punch. No other man had ever caused this kind of instantaneous response in her. In her previous relationships, the attraction had developed more slowly, beginning with shared interests, friendship. This was . . . ridiculous. Pulling a box of crackers from the shelf, she walked back to the counter.

"Are you hungry? The kids and I had a fast-food picnic in front of the TV while we watched you on the six o'clock news. I took the liberty of chilling the champagne."

Without waiting for a reply, she moved away to get glasses. She had a plan. She'd better concentrate on it, instead of on the way he made her feel when he looked at her. Ply the man with champagne and caviar, then give him the bad news about Mrs. Winthrop.

She sent the cork shooting to the ceiling and poured the bubbling liquid into glasses. Handing one to Chase, she asked, "Is this your regular diet, or do you keep it on hand just for special occasions?"

He picked up his glass. "This was a birthday gift from my mother."

His neutral tone had Sunny studying him. "You look exhausted. Drink up. You put in quite a day."

Chase searched her eyes. When he saw understanding, something quiet moved through him, and his tension eased. Odd that he hadn't noticed the color of her eyes before. They were the blue green shade of shallow water over a reef. Quiet and inviting. They turned lighter when she laughed, he recalled. And he could imagine how in passion they would darken to the almost black shade of a storm-churned sea.

The instant he realized the direction his thoughts were taking, he said, "I didn't expect to find you here. What happened to Mrs. Winthrop?"

Sunny refilled their glasses and took a quick sip of her own for courage. "I fired her."

"You *what?*"

Sunny found the flash of anger in his eyes all the more potent in comparison to the ice in his tone. She set her glass carefully on the counter. "I can explain." She held up a hand. "And if you're thinking of getting violent, I have to warn you. I know karate."

"I never get violent."

The clipped way he said the words made her raise her chin. "I don't believe you."

He studied her, noting the defiance in her eyes, the courage in the set of her shoulders. She wasn't about to give an inch. Admiration mixed with his anger. He certainly had every right to be angry, he reminded himself. But even as he thought it, the feeling began to fade. She looked too much like Joan of Arc being led to the stake. Finally he gave up and shrugged. "We're even then. I don't believe you know karate."

The smile started in her eyes, and by the time her lips curved, it had lit up her whole face. Chase simply stared at her. Where had he gotten the idea she wasn't beautiful?

"You're right," Sunny said. "But it's always one of my New Year's resolutions. Every year." She folded her arms on the counter. "I suppose you'd like an explanation about Mrs. Winthrop." At his nod, she launched into the presentation she'd been composing and revising all day long. Surely he would see that The Growing Place was infinitely preferable to Mrs. Winthrop.

When she finished, she held her breath. Nothing in his expression indicated what he was thinking. As the silence stretched between them, she picked up the jar of caviar and began to fiddle with the top.

"Of course, I know it's none of my business," she finally said.

"No, it's not." A smile softened the harshness of the words. "But I can see you care about my niece and nephew. Perhaps you were right to take them with you, instead of leaving them with Mrs. Winthrop."

Encouraged, Sunny nodded. "She was so cold. You must have seen it when you interviewed her."

"Well, I didn't interview her."

Sunny's eyes widened. "You didn't?"

"I..." Chase paused for a moment and frowned. Why was he feeling defensive all of a sudden? "Her references were excellent. And I could hardly meet with her personally when I was still in Boston."

"Oh, of course not," Sunny said. "But wait till you see her. You won't be able to leave the children with her. Not even for a minute. And Heather has plenty of room for them. So." Raising her glass, she beamed a smile at him. "It's all settled, then."

Chase removed the glass from her hands and set it back on the counter. "Not by a long shot. Jason and Emma are used to having a nanny, and I decided that hiring one is the most practical and efficient solution to my problem."

"You feel that the children are a problem?"

"No." Chase frowned again. "That's not what I meant. The problem is me. David and Laura appointed me as Emma and Jason's guardian, and I don't know anything at all about raising children."

"Love is the most important thing in raising children," Sunny said.

"Yes. Well..." Now he was feeling guilty. Why was it he was always struggling to keep his advantage with this woman? "Surely you aren't naive enough to believe that love solves everything."

Sunny met his gaze squarely. "I'd choose it over efficiency and practicality any day."

"Well, love can't always be depended on. A nanny will provide the children with the stability they need right now."

"Stability?" Wrinkling her nose, Sunny tried a new tack. "Surely you can give them that. And let Heather provide the fun. A nanny is so proper and impersonal. Do you really want them to grow up detached from life?"

Chase's eyebrows lifted. "I was raised by a nanny."

"Whoops."

The genuine dismay in her eyes had his lips twitching. "Not that I see myself as a stellar result of the process. Nevertheless, there is something to be said for order and discipline in a child's life."

Sunny stared at him for a minute. "You sound just like Captain Von Trapp in *The Sound of Music*."

Smiling, Chase inclined his head. "There's a fine example. He hired a nanny for his children, and it worked out just fine."

"Well, yes, but she was different. And he had to marry her to keep her. Believe me, I don't see you and Mrs. Winthrop hiking off over the Alps to happy-ever-after land."

Chase threw back his head and laughed, filling the kitchen with a rich, warm sound. Suddenly Sunny wanted to join in. Alight with laughter, his eyes were the color of fog. The kind that held secrets. She'd always found people with secrets fascinating. But that had always gotten her into trouble. She wasn't even aware that her fingers had tightened on the jar of caviar until the top popped off, spilling some of the contents on the counter.

She glanced down at it, then back at Chase. "I'm sorry. Will it go to waste?"

"Not if we eat it. It's supposed to go well with champagne."

Sunny watched as he broke a cracker and dipped one corner into the jar. She was reaching for the box, intending to follow suit, when he offered her the one he'd prepared.

"You first." As he inserted the cracker into her mouth, his fingers brushed her chin. Waves of heat rippled through her right down to her toes. For a second she couldn't move. She could only absorb. Then slowly she chewed, swallowed and tasted nothing.

"Do you like it?" Chase asked.

Like? No, like was much too tame a word to describe what she'd just experienced.

Chase's eyes narrowed. Could her skin possibly be paler than it had been only seconds ago? And he'd have sworn her eyes were darker now. He saw the confused panic in their depths. "You don't have to like it," he hastened to assure her. "I hate the stuff. It's my personal opinion that it tastes like day-old fish bait."

Sunny watched in horror as he walked to the sink and began to tip the contents of the jar down the sink.

"No. Please. I barely tasted it."

He brought the jar back and set it in front of her. "You're sure?"

"Definitely. I want to be able to recall every detail so that I can remember it later." She dipped in a cracker the way she'd seen him do. "I use imagery and visualization techniques. In my business."

"I beg your pardon?"

"Successful athletes and professional businessmen do it all the time."

Chase blinked. "Eat caviar?"

"No." Sunny smiled as she shook her head. "They picture their goal. Picture what it will be like to make that shot or close a million-dollar deal. And they use as much sensory detail as possible." She turned her hands over, palms up. "That's where the caviar and champagne come in. Details. I want to be able to remember the taste. Then I can call it up later when I'm doing my exercises."

"And your goal is what, exactly?" Chase asked.

"I am determined to make Service with a Smile such a huge success I can sell franchises and become a millionaire." She waved a hand. "That's a long-term goal, of course. And to reach it I need to increase my profit margins each year. So to improve my motivation, I try to visualize just what I'll be able to do when I'm rich and successful."

"Like eat caviar and drink champagne?"

"Exactly." She beamed at him across the counter. "The food of the rich and famous."

She was certainly unusual, he thought as she closed her eyes, drew in a deep breath and then let it out. She bit into the cracker. Thirty seconds stretched into a minute while he waited, watching her face. Her skin was flawless except for the sprinkle of freckles across her nose. And it was as soft as it looked. He recalled exactly how it had felt when his fingers had brushed against it. At first the coolness of silk, and then the quick rush of heat. What had she called it? Sensory detail?

His gaze lowered to her mouth. Her lips looked as soft as her skin. And they were damp. If he tasted them now, there would be the salty flavor of the caviar, and what else? He only had to lean forward . . . He caught himself when he was only inches away. From what? Kissing her? A woman he hardly knew?

When Sunny opened her eyes, she found herself staring into his. It wasn't laughter she saw, nor the quick, hot flash of anger she'd seen earlier. It was something much more potent. She felt her own response start in her stomach, an edgy, burning sensation that radiated right to the tips of her fingers. Her gaze dropped to his mouth. His lips were narrow, masculine. They wouldn't be soft when they pressed against hers. And they wouldn't ask, but take.

For a moment neither of them moved. They simply wondered. Chase was the first to draw away. Sunny immediately felt the coolness that even that slight separation caused.

"Well?" he asked.

She stared blankly at him.

"Will you be able to remember it?"

Will I ever be able to forget it? she wondered.

"The caviar?" Chase prompted.

She quickly swallowed the bite she'd been holding in her mouth. Then she shivered and reached for the champagne to wash the taste away. "Unforgettable. But you're right. Fish bait. Caviar is definitely not going to help me get rich." She set her glass down and tried to ignore that her body was still throbbing with a thousand little pulses.

Slowly she drew in a deep breath. She was not here to taste caviar or drink champagne. Or to let Chase Monroe III . . . what? Seduce her with a look?

"About the children," she began, and was pleased to find her voice sounded almost normal. "Is there any way I can convince you to give my friend Heather's place a chance?"

"No. I have to do what I feel is best for them."

"Yes." This was something she understood, and she had no argument against it. "Well—" she placed a card on the counter as she slid off the stool "—if you rehire Mrs. Winthrop and she doesn't work out, call me."

He watched her walk away. "Aren't you forgetting something?"

She turned in the archway to the hall. "What?"

"The reason you came here this morning. To increase your profit margins."

Sunny's eyes narrowed. "You said Mrs. Winthrop would be handling all that."

"I could tell her to use Service with a Smile."

"Why?"

He shrugged. "It would be practical and efficient if she did. That way she could spend more time with the children. Besides, I seem to be fresh out of champagne and caviar."

She folded her arms across her chest and met his eyes squarely. "An interview about my uncle will not be part of the deal."

"Why not?"

"Your TV station's ex-star reporter has already had a field day with him."

Chase sipped his champagne and rested one elbow on the counter. "Leo Caldwell was a state senator. It goes with the territory. Especially if you use your office as a means to acquire a personal fortune."

Sunny crossed the distance between them in a flash. "No one ever proved he took those kickbacks."

"He accepted a deal with the prosecutors. Some might construe that as an admission of guilt."

She jabbed a finger into his chest. "You can construe it any way you want. But you won't be putting a word of that garbage on the nightly news. Not if I can help it."

Hadn't he wondered what her eyes would look like heated by passion? They were magnificent. Once again he thought of Joan of Arc, this time in battle.

She jabbed him again. "He's an old man. He accepted that deal because he was tired of fighting, and he's spending the next ten years in prison. Can't you be satisfied with that and leave him in peace?"

Chase stared at her. Loyalty was something he admired, even when it was misdirected. "You can't believe your uncle is completely innocent."

"Guilty or innocent, it's not up to the press to convict him. And that's exactly what Jeff Miller tried to do."

Chase saw the flash of pain in her eyes. Because he wanted to touch her, he shoved his hands into his pockets. "Jeff Miller doesn't work for us anymore. And we've hired someone to replace him starting next week. I don't want to interview your uncle on the nightly news. I just want to talk to him about a book I'm writing on white-collar crime."

"No interview. My uncle is through with the press."

"Unless the price is right."

"That's not true!"

Chase said nothing. He knew for a fact that Leo Caldwell was working on a deal for the rights to his biography that might bring him seven figures. But Chase would have been willing to bet that Sunny knew nothing about it.

"Are you two mad at each other?"

They turned as one to find Jason staring at them from the archway to the hall.

"No." Sunny was the first to answer.

"Did we wake you up?" Chase asked as he lifted the little boy into his arms.

Jason shook his head. "A bad dream."

"I'll tuck you in." Chase glanced back at Sunny. "You'll wait?"

"Sure."

She waited fifteen minutes before she walked down the hall to the children's bedroom. Fully clothed, Chase was lying facedown on Jason's bed sound asleep. The other bed held Emma, curled into a ball with the covers tangled around her. The only sound was their gentle, even breathing.

He loved them, she thought, as she moved closer. It was clear in the way his arm lay protectively across Jason. *Sweet* was the word that came to mind, and the minute it did, Sunny shook her head. Chase Monroe was definitely not a sweet man. Ruthless, yes. And devilishly handsome. Her gaze moved from his rumpled hair down the long lean length of him. Even asleep, he rated a second look.

Chase Monroe was not what she'd expected. Perhaps it would be easier to deal with the footloose bachelor she'd pictured in her mind. Not that she'd had much evidence to back the image up. In his occasional appearances in the society columns, his name had never been linked with the same woman twice. In fact, it often appeared alone. Surprising.

And so was his passion. Perhaps because he kept it well hidden beneath that control he had most of the time. She recalled the anger she'd seen in his eyes over the firing of Mrs. Winthrop.

And even more surprising was the sense of humor she'd glimpsed more than once.

But he was also a reporter. She couldn't allow herself to forget that. If she hadn't encouraged her uncle to give Jeff Miller that series of interviews, Leo Caldwell might not have felt pressured to make a deal with the prosecutors. If she was smart, she'd give Chase Monroe III a wide berth.

But before she left, she pulled a blanket up over him and turned off the overhead light.

THE PHONE WAS RINGING when Sunny let herself into the carriage house. The only light came from the small goose-necked lamp that Hector used in his work space near the computer.

That was why she nearly jumped out of her skin when she heard the flapping of wings and felt the quick pinch of bird claws on her shoulder. Forcing herself to stay perfectly still, she waited until her heart eased its way out of her throat and reminded herself that the bird was more frightened than she was.

"Gracie, sweetheart." Very gently she ran her finger over the crown of the parakeet's head. "You should be in your cage."

"Buenos días," Gracie said.

"Ah, now I understand." Keeping a firm but gentle grip on the bird, Sunny nudged the light switch on with her free elbow and walked toward the cage. "Hector's been teaching you Spanish, and you repaid him by flying away? Bad girl, Gracie."

The bird replied in more Spanish. Sunny recognized a phrase that Hector often said when he lost something in the computer. Her eyebrows rose as she stuck her hand through the door and waited for Gracie to hop onto her perch.

"You keep that up, and I'm going to have to wash your mouth out with soap. And maybe Hector's, too."

It was only as she covered the cage and turned to the phone that she realized it was no longer ringing. And no message had been left on the machine. With a frown, she glanced at her watch. Midnight. It wouldn't have been a customer. Who, then?

Yawning, she began pulling herself up the ladder to the loft. Wrong number, perhaps. When it rang again, she dropped to the floor and grabbed the receiver. Static poured into her ear. Then a muffled voice asked, "Sunny, is that you?"

"Who is this?"

"Uncle Leo."

"You don't sound like yourself. Are you all right?"

"Sure, sure."

Sunny pressed the receiver closer to her ear, and a fresh wave of static came over the line.

"...more money. Can you..." Sunny listened to more static "...insurance?"

"Uncle Leo, I can barely hear you. The connection—"

The static stopped. "I hate to ask. But I need more money for my appeal. Can you get your hands on some?"

"No. I gave you everything in my savings account."

"Can you borrow on the business?"

"No. It's a service business. I have next to nothing in assets. We discussed this before. Don't you remember?"

"Insurance—" Whatever else her Uncle Leo said was muffled by more static.

"Uncle Leo, are you still there? Are you all right?"

When the static cleared, all she heard was a dial tone. She replaced the receiver, then stared at it for a minute. He'd sounded so strange. Desperate almost. Uncle Leo was never desperate. Even when he'd asked her for the initial ten thousand dollars, he'd assured her he'd be able to pay her back very soon. It was merely a matter of liquidating a few of his assets.

And how in the world had he gotten permission to use a phone at this hour of the night? Even in the federal prison facility that Leo had been sent to, there were still a lot of restrictions. It wasn't at all the country club that some members of the press liked to call it.

Then again, Uncle Leo had a way about him. Her lips curved in a smile. Even in a federal prison, it seemed. When a sudden yawn overtook her, she made her way to the ladder. In the morning, she'd call his attorneys and ask them to check it out. Maybe they could start earning some of the money he was paying them.

3

THE POUNDING brought Sunny out of a sound sleep into a cranky, half-conscious state. How could she possibly be caught in a stampede? The closest she'd ever been to a ranch was in the movies. One deep breath told her she wasn't in a theater. No popcorn.

She was about to burrow under her pillow when she felt a tug on her hair and claws digging into her scalp. Gracie. Oh, she was home all right. By the time she got her eyes open, the parakeet was flying over the railing that separated the loft from the rest of the carriage house.

"Damn!" Sunny muttered. She had a very clear memory of putting Gracie in her cage before she went to bed. Struggling into a sitting position, she tried to focus on her alarm clock. Six-thirty?

The pounding increased in volume. Sunny flattened the palms of her hands against her ears. Could this be a hangover? After only one glass of champagne? Aiming a dark look at the door, she rolled off her futon and crawled on all fours to her dresser.

When the drawer stuck halfway out, she whacked it with the side of her hand and yanked. It gave an inch. A new dresser, she promised herself. Just as soon as she increased her profit margins. Grabbing yellow sweats, she pulled them on, then the matching shirt. And finally she began the search for her slippers.

The latest pair she'd bought were impossible to lose. She'd found them in the children's department, and they looked like large, overstuffed cats, complete with whiskers. One was peeking out from the end of her futon. The other she snagged from under the dresser. Stuffing her feet into them, she tied her hair back with a ribbon and hurried down the ladder.

The moment Sunny opened the door Emma launched herself into Sunny's arms. Returning the little girl's hug, she put her hand up to shade her eyes and squinted at Chase. He was the last person she'd expected to see. Even with her eyes barely open, she noted that his jacket had the soft, expensive look of cashmere. His striped shirt was crisply ironed, and the crease in the gray slacks that covered his long legs had a military preciseness. The whole outfit made Sunny feel as if she'd just tumbled, fully fluffed, out of a dryer.

Chase stared right back at her. She reminded him of Raggedy Ann. Except... His gaze dropped lower. Even in loose-fitting sweats, there was no mistaking the length of her legs. And good Lord, were those cats on her feet?

"You're wearing cats on your feet," Jason said, removing his thumb from his mouth and stooping to pet them.

"They just look like cats. I wear them to scare the mice," Sunny explained.

"Mice?" Jason glanced around the room with interest. "Where are they?"

"Hiding. They don't dare come out while I'm wearing these slippers." She stamped her feet up and down. "They're too frightened."

Jason looked at the slippers, then up at Sunny. "Can I wear them?"

"Jason . . ." Chase began.

But Sunny had already stepped out of the stuffed cats. In a flash, Jason was shuffling down the length of the room in them.

Chase's gaze followed his nephew. "You're very good with them."

"It's not hard," Sunny said.

Chase watched her carry Emma to the corner of the room that seemed to serve as a living space. A short counter divided a small kitchen from a sectional couch set against the opposite walls. A pitcher of roses on a low table echoed one of the colors in the plaid fabric covering the couch. A sunny yellow rug highlighted another. The counters held various appliances that looked as if they were frequently used. The whole effect was inviting, especially in contrast with the stark, businesslike appearance of the rest of the large room.

"How long have you lived here?" he asked.

"I moved in the day I graduated from college and got a teaching job. Uncle Leo lent me the money to fix it up. He knew I needed to move out of my mom's house." Sunny paused to give him a wry smile. "Mom wasn't quite as understanding. So we compromised. I just moved away as far as the back lawn."

"Your mom lives in the house I drove past?"

"She did until she got remarried last year and moved to Florida. Now my aunts live there. Would you like a cola?" Sunny bent over to pull a can out of her refrigerator.

Chase turned and found himself staring at the smooth, white skin that was revealed when her sweatshirt hiked up from her waist. Swallowing, he tried to relieve the sudden dryness in his throat.

"The kids can have some, can't they? I'm out of juice."

"Sure." He watched her divide the cola into four glasses. "You have something against coffee?"

Sunny grinned. "It takes time to brew. I have to get my caffeine fix much quicker than that." After handing a glass to Emma, she drained the contents of her own.

Gracie chose that moment to land on Chase's head. Sunny grabbed his hand.

"What the hell—"

"Don't make any quick moves. You'll scare her," Sunny said as she coaxed the bird onto her finger.

"Scare who?" Chase asked.

"This is Gracie, my parakeet."

Abandoning the cat slippers, Jason raced down the length of the room. "Can I pet her?"

"If you're very careful." She settled Emma on the floor next to Jason and squatted down so that she was facing them. "She'll fly away if you make any sudden moves." Sunny ran her finger gently along the bird's head.

"*Buenos días,*" Gracie said.

"She talks." Jason stared wide-eyed at the bird.

"She speaks Spanish?" Chase asked.

"Courtesy of Hector," Sunny said in a dry tone.

Chase glanced up at the loft. "Who's Hector?" It hadn't occurred to him that she might live with someone.

"My assistant. He developed an accounting program for Service with a Smile that he was able to use as his master's thesis at the university. Lucky for me, he's decided to continue on for his doctorate. Here, Emma, give me your hand, and I'll show you how to pet Gracie."

Chase watched her do just that. The children were enchanted. And not just by the bird. Jason had asked for Sunny the moment he woke up. Emma had begun to cry the moment he'd explained that they wouldn't be seeing her today. That was when Jason had suddenly become more interested in his thumb than in his bowl of Bluegaloos.

It wouldn't do for the children to become too dependent on her. At least that was what he'd decided in the wee hours of the morning when he'd awakened in Jason's bed. Weren't their lives already complicated enough? Sunny Caldwell promised to complicate things even more. And yet he was here.

Chase watched her as she sat on the floor, one leg tucked underneath her and the other extended. The sweats were hiked up to her knee, revealing a length of bare calf, an ankle and foot as slender and delicate as the rest of her. Once more he felt the stir of desire, this time sharper, edgier. Why was it he couldn't be around her for more than a few minutes without wanting to touch her?

Sunny noticed the tension the moment she looked at him. It was in the line of his shoulder, in the grim set of his mouth. He looked . . . isolated. Did he want to join them? He certainly wasn't dressed to sit on the floor and pet a bird.

Settling Gracie on Jason's fingers, she rose and walked toward him. "I know exactly what you're thinking," she said.

"You do?"

"You're wondering if you've fallen down the rabbit hole or stepped through the looking glass." But when she laid her hand on his arm, it wasn't an answering smile she saw in his eyes.

The moment Sunny touched him, Chase forgot what he was thinking. She was so close. He could smell her scent, fresh, like spring flowers. Unable to stop himself, he reached out to touch a curl, winding it around his finger.

Sunny tried to ignore the way her heart began to slam against her ribs. For the first time she became aware of how much taller he was. She had to tilt her head quite a way back to see his throat and the pulse hammering there. His hand on her hair was so light. It had to be the caffeine that was making her feel out of breath. As soon as she got rich, she would buy herself a juicer and give up her morning injection of cola. In the meantime she put some effort into breathing and said, "I'll bet you're wondering what's going to happen next."

His gaze dropped to her lips and lingered for a moment before returning to her eyes. "I know what I want to happen next."

Sunny's mind went completely blank. She heard Gracie say something, but she couldn't make out the words. She recalled exactly what she'd felt the night before in his kitchen. But this time what moved through her was sharper, more urgent. She wanted to step forward almost as much as she wanted to step back. Chase's fingers pressing at the back of her neck took the decision out of her hands.

His lips were inches from hers when Jason giggled. The sound seemed to come from very far away.

"What the hell!" the boy shouted as Gracie took flight.

Sunny pressed her hand against Chase's chest and tried to gather her scattered thoughts. Then she stared in horror as the bird dropped a deposit on the sleeve of Chase's jacket.

"Whoops," she said as she backed around the edge of the counter. "Don't move. I'll get something to sponge it off. Soda water. It won't leave a stain."

"Don't worry about it," Chase said, wondering if he should thank the bird or curse it. He carefully removed the jacket and folded it on the counter. "I'll get it cleaned."

Sunny gave the sleeve another stricken look. "It's cashmere, isn't it? I'll pay for the cleaning."

"What the hell," Jason said again as Gracie landed on his head briefly.

Chase tried to disguise his laugh as a cough. And he might have succeeded if he hadn't looked at Sunny. Her eyes were filled with such merriment, such understanding, that he threw back his head and let the laugh escape. They were all still gasping for breath when Hector walked in, skateboard in one hand and boom box in the other.

"What's so funny?" he asked.

While Sunny explained and made the introductions, Chase used the time to size up Hector Rodriguez. The young man stood about six foot, and wore his hair pulled back into a ponytail. He had one pierced ear, and a tattoo decorated his left forearm. A quick glance at Jason had Chase inwardly groaning. The boy was taking in every detail. But Hector's handshake was firm, and the eyes behind the wire-rimmed glasses were intelligent and friendly.

"Hector's my number cruncher," Sunny was telling the children.

"How do you crunch numbers?" Jason asked.

"With my computer. C'mon, I'll show you."

As Sunny watched them cross the room to the space Hector called his own, she spoke in a low tone to Chase. "He's really a very nice young man, even though he doesn't . . . I mean, just because he . . ."

"Doesn't carry a briefcase or wear a suit? Relax, Sunny. I don't always wear one myself."

She saw the gleam of amusement in his eyes and felt heat flood her face. Did he have to remind her? Would he never let her forget?

"You're very loyal, aren't you?" Chase asked.

"I've never thought much about it."

His eyes narrowed fractionally. "No, I don't believe you do. Now, suppose we talk about why I came over here this morning."

"Of course." It was with a feeling of relief that Sunny turned to open a drawer. "I showed you this yesterday." She placed it in front of him on the counter. "Basically it's a checklist, much easier than writing everything down. And it encourages accuracy. See, if you want catsup, for example, you have to check a brand and a size."

"I didn't come here to order groceries."

"But I thought . . ." A faint frown creased her brow. "That was what we were discussing last night when Jason interrupted." She fisted her hands and placed them on her hips. "Unless you still think I'm going to get you that interview . . ."

"No, I didn't come to discuss your uncle, either." He glanced over at the other end of the room. The children stood at Hector's side, totally engrossed in the computer. "The kids asked for you the moment they woke up this morning."

"Emma spoke?"

"No, she cried. In fact, she didn't stop crying until I promised that we'd come over here." What he didn't say, didn't even want to think too closely about, was that he had also awakened with Sunny Caldwell on his mind.

"I'm sorry." Sunny laid a hand on his arm. "But it's not just me she's crying about. It's the whole situation."

"I'm worried about Jason, too. He's so...so good all the time. He used to run his parents ragged. And he's so serious. The first time he's laughed since the funeral was when you came to the apartment yesterday, and now again this morning."

"It's going to take time for them to adjust. Everything has changed so quickly."

She was only saying what he'd already told himself. Why did hearing someone else say it help so much? "I've decided not to rehire Mrs. Winthrop yet. I want to give your friend, Heather Kelly, a try."

"You do?" The smile lit up her whole face. "You won't be sorry." She glanced at her watch. "I'll have to change, and then I'll walk you over. She'll want to talk to you before the rest of the children arrive."

Hector stopped her on her race for the ladder. "Bad news. I'm going to have to draw on your personal line of credit again," he said.

"Do I have enough?"

"For this week."

She patted him on the arm. "Go ahead."

"Sunny."

She glanced back at him from the third rung of the ladder.

"Your credit line isn't bottomless, you know."

She smiled. "Think positive, Hector."

With a sigh, Hector moved to the refrigerator to get a can of soda.

"Problem?" Chase asked.

Hector shrugged before he opened the can and took a long swallow. "What she needs is an infusion of cash. If she gets a few more customers like you with deep pockets, she'll be all right."

"So there *is* a problem."

Hector met his gaze steadily. "Not that it's any of your business."

"You brought it up. And you strike me as being discreet."

Slowly Hector grinned. "I guess I did. I've read about you in the papers, and I've seen you on TV a couple of times. Back when the symphony was in trouble. I figure you're a straight shooter." He glanced up at the loft. "She wouldn't be happy that I'm talking to you."

Chase said nothing, and after a moment Hector continued, "She's too softhearted for her own good. She insists on carrying thirty of her original customers on credit. Most of them live on social security. She buys their groceries and bills them once a month. Refuses to charge interest." He shook his head. "It's bad policy, but she won't change the deal she made with them. Says they're responsible for her success."

"Doesn't the business have a wide enough profit margin to carry them?" Chase asked.

"It did until her uncle Leo went to jail. Now she feels obligated to step into his shoes and take care of her family. She's determined to keep that mansion of his so he'll have a home when he gets out. Luckily the rent from the day-care center covers the expenses on the place. But she had to move her two aunts into her mom's house. Old Leo was taking care of them on his senator's salary. Now Sunny helps them with the rent. Of course, they don't know about it." Hector took a long drink of his cola. "The amazing thing is that it was all working out okay until she lent her uncle ten thousand dollars for his appeal."

"Are you sure about that?"

"I wrote the check myself."

Chase shook his head. "No, are you sure it was for an appeal?"

Hector nodded.

"Uncle Chase! Sunny! Watch us scare the mice away!"

Hand in hand, Jason and Emma were stomping up and down the room, each wearing one of the cat slippers.

Sunny popped her head over the railing of the loft. "Good work."

"Are there really mice in here?" Chase asked Hector.

"A few." Hector waved an arm. "A hundred years ago this place was a stable. Sunny's scared to death of mice."

"Why on earth doesn't she get a real cat or set some traps?"

"A cat might hurt Gracie, and a trap might actually kill one of the little critters." Hector leaned over to pull another cola out of the refrigerator. "You want one of these?"

"Yeah." Chase sighed. "I think I'm going to need it."

"Well, you two look as though you've hit it off," Sunny said as she stepped off the ladder and joined them.

"We've been discussing your financial problems," Chase said.

"Hector?" She scowled at her assistant.

The young man shrugged and folded his arms across his chest. "Hey, somebody has to talk some sense into you. You're not paying any attention to your accountant."

Sunny glanced at her watch. "I'll deal with you later." To Chase, she said, "C'mon. We have to get over to Heather's."

"HERE, HAVE SOME TEA," Marnie said. "Your aunt Alma has focused her culinary genius on creating this new blend. It's supposed to be very soothing."

Sunny took the cup and sipped it absently.

"Sugar?" Marnie offered.

"No." Sunny glanced down and wrinkled her nose at the anemic-looking liquid. "Sugar's not going to help this. It tastes like dried eucalyptus leaves."

"Oh, no." Marnie took a tentative sip and shivered. "It tastes like day-old kitty litter to me. I'm definitely going to have to find something else for Alma to do." Setting her cup on the tray, she studied Sunny for a moment. "You're worrying too much about those children. Relax. They're going to love it at The Growing Place."

"Yes, but, the problem is whether their uncle will love taking them there, picking them up at five, then dealing with dinner and baths and story time."

"You'll find a way to make it all work out."

"No." Sunny sat on the arm of a chair. "I can't do that."

"Why not?"

"Because it will be better if I don't see them again."

Marnie's eyebrows rose. "Better for whom?"

Sunny stood and began to pace. "Better for them and for me. I've given it a lot of thought. Those children have already lost so much. It won't do them any good if they become too dependent on me. They have to learn to adjust to a new life with their uncle. If I keep seeing them, it'll only make everything more complicated." Sunny paused to straighten the lace doily on the back of the chair. When she glanced up, Marnie was smiling at her.

"You like him, don't you?"

"No. Well, yes." The lace doily dropped to the floor. She stooped to pick it up and slapped it back on the chair. "Whether or not I like Chase Monroe is beside the point. It would be wrong for me to get involved with him or the children."

Marnie's smile widened.

Sunny frowned at her. "What?"

"You're already involved with those children. You can't help yourself."

"Well, I don't want to be. I've waited a long time to be able to concentrate on my business. I need to focus all my energy on increasing my customer base." She pointed an accusing finger at her aunt. "That was the plan when you talked me into mailing Chase that brochure. I know how time-consuming children can be."

Marnie shook her head. "You're thinking about your father again."

"Maybe." Sunny walked to the window and looked out at the carriage house. "I know that if he hadn't spent so much time with Mom and me, he might have realized his dream before he died."

"Do you really think he would have traded a patent on one of those inventions of his for one moment of the time he spent with you and your mom?" Marnie raised a hand to ward off whatever Sunny would have said in reply and picked up the remote control. "I can't argue the point right now. 'Gallagher's Dream' is on."

Sunny directed her scowl at the television screen. There was no point in trying to convince Aunt Marnie, anyway. The person she had to convince was herself. And she had.

As the familiar theme music swelled and filled the room, Sunny watched a series of vignettes flash across the screen. The Gallagher family. First Jack, the graying but charming and ever-smiling patriarch who had risen from immigrant boxing champion to owner of an international hotel chain.

Marnie sighed. "Now there's a man. But I suppose you prefer one of the younger hunks."

Sunny didn't comment as the screen split in two to accommodate Jack Gallagher's lean and handsome sons. Michael, the smooth sophisticate, who during the three years of the series's successful run had seduced and discarded women like wads of used tissue. And Rafe, the ne'er-do-well with the heart of gold who never failed to rescue his family from scrapes and who had an amazing ability to leap behind the wheel of his Jaguar without opening the door or wrinkling his tuxedo.

"This is my favorite part," Marnie said, as the theme music turned suddenly slow and sultry. And though Sunny had seen the introduction to the show many times before, she found herself watching once more as Lila McIntyre went into action as Mariah Gallagher. In the first shot, she was in the corporate offices making love to one of her male secretaries. When Lila McIntyre had joined the show in its second season, "Gallagher's Dream" had shot to the top of the ratings, and it had remained there ever since. In the next vignette, Lila wore nothing but a red feather boa that someone off camera was obligingly spinning her out of. At the very last moment, the screen faded to a commercial.

"She's really something," Marnie said.

"She's certainly done her bit to change the image of the American wife and mother."

"Did you know she's Chase's mother?"

Sunny turned to stare at her aunt. "You're kidding." Her gaze switched to the teapot. "Either that or Aunt Alma put more than dried eucalyptus leaves in that tea."

"I read it in *Who's Who* the last time I was at the library. Lila McIntyre was married to Chase's father for less than a year. When they divorced, he got custody of Chase, and right after that her career really took off. Amazing, don't you think?"

Amazing wasn't the word Sunny would have chosen. Unbelievable, perhaps. She stared at the television and tried to find some resemblance between Chase and the actress who played Mariah Gallagher. "She doesn't look old enough to be his mother."

"Plastic surgery," Marnie said.

Sunny shot her a look. "Did you read that in *Who's Who?*"

"No. She admitted it on all the talk shows after she posed for a centerfold last year."

"Chase's mother posed for a centerfold?"

"And she was gorgeous. Or at least that's what they said on the talk shows."

Without warning, the image of Chase walking down the hall nude flashed into Sunny's mind. Like mother, like son. She started to giggle.

"What's so funny?" Marnie asked.

"Nothing." But she had to bite down hard on her cheek to forestall a second wave of laughter. When she could trust herself to speak, she said, "I'd better go. I have some orders to check over."

Marnie kept her eyes glued to the television set as Mariah burst into Jack Gallagher's office. "You'll feel a lot better after you call Chase and check on the children."

"I'm not going to call Chase," Sunny said, hurrying out of the room to ensure she had the last word on the subject.

CHASE PUNCHED in the numbers and waited while the phone rang four times. The moment he heard Hector's voice, he knew he'd gotten Sunny's answering machine again. Where was she? A glance at his watch told him it had been less than ten minutes since he made his last call. He was about to hang up when he heard a click followed by Sunny's voice. "Hello."

"Sunny."

"Chase. Hello."

"I've been trying to reach you for over an hour."

"Is there a problem?"

"Two problems. One of them is hiding under her bed. The other one is sucking his thumb on top of his. They're not going to bed until they see you. And I think they're hungry."

"Oh?"

"I picked up a pizza on the way home from Heather's. Jason insisted on getting pepperoni and mushrooms. He neglected to mention that Emma won't eat either one. Then he wolfed down three slices and threw up."

"Children are wonderful, aren't they?"

He heard the smile in her voice and felt some of his tension ease. "I've heard they have their moments."

Sunny began to twist the phone cord around her finger. "You're not thinking of throwing in the towel and rehiring Mrs. Winthrop?"

"I'd do more than think about it if it wasn't for one thing."

"Oh?"

"The look on their faces when I picked them up at The Growing Place."

For the first time that day, Sunny felt the tension she'd been feeling begin to dissolve. "It went all right, then?"

"Heather and the children were certainly pleased. But I still have two hungry mouths to feed, and nothing to tempt them with but stale crackers and dead champagne. I called to see if you'll take me on as a customer."

Sunny hesitated for only a second as she thought fleetingly of her earlier resolve. But she couldn't turn her back on two hungry children, could she? "I'll pick up some emergency rations on my way over."

"ONCE UPON A TIME, there lived a princess who had everything she wanted except for—"

"This is a sissy story, I can tell," Jason said, sitting cross-legged at the foot of the bed.

"There's a prince in the story, too," Sunny assured him.

"Does he carry a gun and blow bad people away?" Jason asked.

"No, but he's very smart, and he does help the princess solve her problem."

Jason frowned as Emma crawled onto Sunny's lap. "What's her problem?"

"She has no gravity. So she floats around like the astronauts do in space."

"Gee, that'd be neat. What's wrong with that?"

"What if you were the only one floating around?" Sunny asked.

Jason inched his way closer to Sunny and Emma. "Okay, how did the prince help her?"

Chase stood watching the cozy scene from the doorway of the bedroom. It had taken Sunny less than an hour to feed the children soup and then convince them to take a bath. Bribe them, actually. The story had been the bait.

It occurred to him that whenever Sunny was around the children, they looked like a family. If he took three steps into the room, he could be a part of it.

"If she doesn't have any gravity, why doesn't she just put rocks in her pockets?" Jason asked. "Or lead in her shoes? I know, she could wear one of those astronaut's suits."

"The story takes place years ago before they made astronaut suits," Sunny explained. "Besides those suits make you look like a sausage. Princesses have to wear pretty dresses and lovely glass slippers, right, Emma?"

The little girl nodded.

"Is the prince going to kiss her? I can't stand mushy stuff," Jason warned as he stretched out on his side and stuck his thumb in his mouth.

A princess with no gravity, Chase mused. An odd affliction, and one he could readily sympathize with. Hadn't he been feeling a little light-headed ever since Sunny Caldwell had walked into his life? Over the years he'd learned the value of making carefully thought-out decisions. Now twice in one day he'd acted impulsively. Against his better judgment, he'd enrolled Jason and Emma in a day-care center. And he'd asked Sunny to come over tonight.

Not that he had any regrets, he thought as he watched her smooth Jason's hair back from his forehead. His gaze lingered on her hands. Those long, slender fingers. What would her touch feel like? he wondered. Would it arouse at the same time it soothed? Inflame at the same time it provided relief?

He frowned slightly at the errant direction his thoughts were taking. The same direction they seemed to take whenever he was around Sunny Caldwell. He'd learned long ago to control his emotions, especially with women. He'd seen his father walk down the aisle too often to ever want to follow in his footsteps. As for his stepbrother, he'd always figured David had been born under a lucky star when it came to women.

Chase forced his gaze from Sunny's hands to her face. A few curls had broken free from the ribbon she'd used to contain them, and he found himself wanting to pull them all loose. His frown deepened. She wasn't like any woman he'd ever been attracted to before. And he couldn't remember a time, not even in the throes of raging adolescent hormones, when he'd allowed himself to fantasize about a woman quite this way. Is this what it felt like to operate without gravity? One thing he knew for sure. If he continued to give in to his impulses around Sunny, he might find out exactly what it would feel like to have those strong, gentle hands move over him.

Sunny knew the instant Chase left the room. Still, she glanced up at the empty doorway. Was he upset? Did he think she was trying to take his place with the children?

For the moment she pushed the worrisome thought aside and concentrated on keeping the story of the light princess exciting enough for Jason. But as soon as she tucked the children in, she hurried out to find him.

He was in the kitchen putting the last of the supper dishes away.

"I'm sorry," she said, walking toward him.

"What for?"

She lifted her hands, then dropped them. "You should be the one telling them stories and tucking them in. I didn't mean to—"

"To what? Help me out? I was the one who called and asked you to come over."

"I shouldn't have. It's not going to help you if the kids become too dependent on me."

He walked around the counter. "Why don't you let me be the judge of that?"

He was close, only a foot away. Sunny controlled the urge to step back. "I've been thinking about it. I mean—" she waved a hand "—you're going to need some help. Fixing their dinner, putting them to bed. And even if you don't have to spend as much time at the station, there could be emergencies." Her nervousness was back, knotting her stomach. It was that quiet way Chase had of looking at her, as if he could read her thoughts.

"You haven't changed your mind about Mrs. Winthrop?" he asked.

"Heavens, no. What you need is my aunt Alma."

"Your aunt Alma?"

"She's the perfect solution. She used to cook and entertain for my uncle Leo. Now she's living in a smaller house. She's . . . well, bored. This would be great for her." Warming to her theme, Sunny began to move around the room. "She can cook." She thought briefly of the eucalyptus tea and hurried on. "More importantly, she loves children."

Chase was only half listening to Sunny ramble on about her aunt Alma's virtues. The other half of his mind was focused on Sunny herself. Her clothes were more subdued than usual tonight. Faded jeans and a plain white T-shirt. She had a certain energy. Perhaps it was because her feelings were so close to the surface. Even now as she spoke so enthusiastically about her aunt, the warmth and loyalty seemed to flow out of her. Was that what drew him? Or was it the cynical reporter in him that couldn't help but wonder how deep those feelings went? Perhaps it was time to find out.

"Well?" Sunny turned to find Chase right behind her. Once again she had to fight the urge to step back. "What do you think about Aunt Alma?"

"I'm not thinking about her at all."

"I wish you would. I can't come over here every night to tuck Emma and Jason in." Sunny could have sworn he hadn't moved, but Chase seemed closer than he had a second ago. The top two buttons of his shirt were open, revealing the smooth tan skin of his throat. She remembered the tan line where his thigh joined his hip and almost lost her train of thought completely. Jason and Emma. Something about . . . Aunt Alma! Clearing her throat, she dragged her eyes from his throat to his eyes. "Aren't you the one who was arguing on the side of practicality and efficiency? Aunt Alma will provide that."

"Fine. Set up an interview for me." This time when he moved forward, she stepped back—smack against the wall.

"You're nervous," he said as he watched her eyes darken with confusion and then with something more tempting.

"No."

He laid a finger gently against the pulse hammering in her throat. "Then why is your heart racing?"

"I'm anxious. About Gracie. My parakeet. I forgot to feed her." But she couldn't move. She could feel each push of her blood against his finger, and it weakened her.

He leaned close enough to brush his lips briefly against hers, then drew back to watch her eyes widen and darken until they matched the color of the sea just before a storm.

"Don't." She tried to press herself into the wall. "It's not a good idea."

"Probably not." She felt the words more than she heard them as his mouth covered hers. Not gently, but with the force and edgy passion she'd expected. And wanted. Before she could think to control her response, she moved her hands to grip his shoulders. Her fingers pressed into the tight band of muscle, pulling him closer. She felt her body heat from the center out.

Sensations raced through her, and she tried desperately to absorb each one. The nip of his teeth on her bottom lip, the pressure of his fingers as they tangled in her hair. The wall was hard at her back, the firm angles of his body pressing equally hard against her. So this was desire, this quick explosion of heat that threatened to consume her.

With a groan, Chase pulled his mouth away from hers. To catch his breath. To grasp at his control. His hands were still trapped in her hair, and her scent still wrapped itself around him. He watched her lips form his name and knew he had to taste her again.

She was so soft. Even crushed against him, she yielded. He could feel his blood pounding against her at each and every contact point, even through layers of clothes. Desire shot through him as an image filled his mind. Quite clearly, he could see himself making love to her, taking her quickly right here against the wall. Outrageous. Unthinkable. Still the image lingered, and his need built. With an oath, he released her and took two quick steps back.

Sunny didn't move. She wasn't at all sure she could. Below her knees, her legs felt like water. Pressing her hands against the wall for support, she opened her eyes to find Chase standing a few feet away. She drew in a deep breath. "Why did you do that?"

Chase stared at her. Why indeed? It was all he could do to keep himself from doing it again.

"Why did you do that?" Her chin lifted as she repeated the question.

"Curiosity."

Sunny's brows snapped together. "Oh, great!" She welcomed the surge of annoyance. With any luck she could fan it into anger. And anger might bring the strength back into her legs. "Suppose the next time you get curious, you leave me out of it." She tested her legs, found they worked and then used them. In the archway, she turned to face him. She was not running away. Certainly not from a kiss that had meant nothing to Chase Monroe III. "What time do you want to see my aunt?"

"Nine o'clock tomorrow morning. Aren't you forgetting something?" When he moved toward her, he saw the wariness in her eyes and the stubborn set of her jaw. Both pleased him. "Your uncle," he said and was even more pleased when she shifted as he reached around her to lift a book off the hall table. "We haven't finished that discussion."

"Oh, yes, we have."

"Here." He handed the book to her. "I'd like you to read this. It will give you some idea of how I approach a subject I'm working on."

Sunny glanced at the title. *The Politics of World Famine.*

"If you still think I'm out to exploit your uncle when you're finished, I'll give up the idea of interviewing him. But I can offer him a substantial sum if he'll see me."

Sunny was halfway out the door when Chase said, "Ten thousand dollars. I'll be waiting for your call."

4

"SUNNY!" MARNIE WAVED at her niece from her sentry position in the window of the den.

Resigned, Sunny closed the door of the carriage house and walked across the lawn. For three days she'd managed to avoid her aunts. But Sunday was her day off. That gave her two choices—hide in the carriage house all day or face the music.

"Welcome, stranger!" Alma said as Sunny entered the room. The older woman sat in a rocker, matching the rhythm of the chair to the in-and-out motion of her crochet hook.

"How about a cup of tea?" Marnie shot Sunny a meaningful look. "It's quite good today."

Alma wrinkled her nose. "If you like the junk they stuff in those teabags."

"We're happy to make do with store-bought," Marnie said as she handed Sunny a cup. "Your new job taking care of Jason and Emma has to come first, Alma."

"How are they?" Sunny asked, perching on the arm of a chair. "The children—"

"Miss you." Alma halted the movement of her rocking chair to point her crochet hook at Sunny. "They want to know when they're going to see you."

"Hector and I are always swamped at the end of the week. We didn't finish the deliveries last night until after nine."

Alma sniffed. "You could have dropped by on your way home. I couldn't get those children in bed until after midnight. Their uncle was out late at a business dinner, and they were worried. Poor things. So many people have abandoned them lately."

"Your aunt Alma really could have used your help, my dear," Marnie said. "I tried to get you on the phone after I saw your van pull into the drive. But all I got was your machine."

Sunny frowned. "You were here all by yourself, weren't you?" Setting her cup on the table, she rose and began to pace. "When I recommended Aunt Alma to Chase, I never thought it would mean you'd be left alone at night." She turned to face Alma. "The next time he asks you to stay late, you let me know. I'll come over to stay with Aunt Marnie."

"There's no need," Marnie said. "I can take care of myself."

"I got the gun out for her before I left," Alma added.

"The *what?*"

"Have some more tea, dear," Marnie said. "Leo bought a gun for us years ago. There were so many nights when he had to stay in Albany and we were alone in that big house of his."

"And he thought you needed a gun? Why didn't he install a security system? Or buy a big dog?"

"Too much trouble," Alma said. "We preferred a gun."

Sunny reached for her cup and drained the contents. Then she sank slowly into her chair. "Have you ever actually fired it?"

"Not at a burglar. But one of these days—" Alma aimed her crochet hook at the ceiling "—pow!" She grinned at Sunny. "Just kidding. We've only used it at the practice range. Marnie's a crack shot."

Marnie beamed at her niece. "I keep telling you you don't have to worry about us."

Sunny stared at her two aunts. "That settles it. I am definitely going to have to pay Uncle Leo a visit this week."

"I'm sure he'll be glad to see you. But you don't have to worry your head about us," Marnie said.

"Or your uncle Leo, either," Alma added.

"I'm not so sure. He called me last Monday. He needs more money for his appeal."

"Nonsense!" Alma said. "Don't you dare give him another cent. You shouldn't have given him that ten thousand dollars to begin with." She waved a hand to keep Sunny from interrupting. "I know you love him. And I know you've got some misguided notion that you're responsible for the length of his sentence just because you arranged the interview with that flashy young reporter. But you're wrong." She pointed her crochet hook at Sunny one last time before she wrapped a piece of lace around it and stuffed it into a bag. "I love my brother, too. But I know him. And the government didn't get all his money. He's got plenty tucked away somewhere."

Marnie nodded her head in agreement. "I can remember at Christmas and Easter when we got candy, Leo always used to hide some of his. Alma and I always ate ours. Every last piece, even if we got sick. Then we'd talk your father into giving us some of his. But Leo always kept his for himself."

"I think you're wrong this time," Sunny said. "He sounded . . . funny. Not like himself at all. And yesterday, he called Mom in Florida to see if she could borrow against the mortgage on this house."

"Well, I hope she had the good sense to say no." Alma reached for her cup, then made a face. "I'm going to have to make a pot of my own tea. You can just taste the chemicals in this stuff."

"She didn't agree to do anything with the mortgage, did she?" Marnie asked.

"It's not that. Mom had to remind him that he holds the mortgage. She'd have to borrow from him." Sunny stood and started to pace again. "How could he forget something like that? Maybe jail is affecting his mind. I've been calling his attorneys all week. They're getting back to me."

Alma snorted. "You won't get a straight answer out of them."

"Make arrangements for Chase to go with you when you visit Leo," Marnie suggested. "I'm sure he'll take care of everything for you. He reminds me so much of Rafe on 'Gallagher's Dream,' just the sort of man you can trust to solve all your problems."

Sunny shook her head in exasperation. "Life is not a soap opera, Aunt Marnie. People don't come bounding out of Jaguars to help you in real life."

"She's got a point," Alma said. "They'd probably catch their bejoobies on the steering wheel if they tried it."

"Besides, Chase is the last person I can ask to help with this. He wants to interview Uncle Leo too. He's even willing to pay ten thousand dollars if Uncle Leo will agree."

"See!" Marnie clapped her hands together. "Then Leo can pay you back the money he owes you. I told you

Chase could solve your problems. Go ahead. Call him."

When Sunny turned to Alma for help, her aunt just shrugged. "For once, I have to agree with my sister."

GRACIE LANDED on her shoulder the moment Sunny let herself into the carriage house.

"You're too smart for your own good," Sunny murmured as she stroked her finger gently across the bird's head. "Shame on you, getting out of your cage like that. Your brain's not supposed to be that big."

"*Buenos días,*" Gracie replied.

"I'm not sure it's so *buenos,*" Sunny muttered as she walked toward the phone. Chase's number was next to it, taped to the wall. She'd put it there two days ago after she'd finished reading his book. It was then she'd decided she had a major problem on her hands.

The book was well written, insightful and quite objective in its presentation of the problems involved in solving the world's hunger problems. But even if it had been biased and sensational, she would still have had a problem. Chase was offering Uncle Leo ten thousand dollars.

Evidently Uncle Leo needed it. How could she refuse to let him know about the offer?

Hands on hips, she stared at Chase's number. But she didn't reach for the phone. Because money wasn't the real problem. Her hesitation about calling Chase Monroe had very little to do with protecting her uncle. It had everything to do with protecting herself.

She could still remember the way she'd felt when he'd kissed her, the desire, the need. And she hadn't wanted him to stop. Tapping her foot on the floor, she frowned, annoyed by her cowardice. What could happen over the phone?

It rang just as she touched it. Startled, she drew in a quick breath, and Gracie flew away. She swore softly, then picked up the receiver. "Service with a Smile."

"You don't sound like you're smiling."

"Chase?" She struggled to prevent the smile and failed. "I was just going to call you. About Uncle Leo."

"Good. We can discuss it at the zoo."

"The zoo?" Wrapping the phone cord around her finger, she watched Gracie land on a square of sunlight on the counter. How long had it been since she'd gone to the zoo?

"I'm desperate. The rain kept us inside all day yesterday, and I think we're going stir-crazy. Jason insisted I call and invite you. He's missed you. Emma, too."

And Sunny had missed the children. More than she was willing to admit.

"It's Sunday, and the zoo's bound to be crowded. I thought two adults would be better than one," Chase continued.

A lot could happen over the phone, Sunny was discovering. The sound of a voice could make a person's skin tingle. Just simple vibrations could conjure up images, feelings.

"*Que sera, sera,*" Gracie chirped.

Sunny stared at the bird. Whatever will be, will be? Well, some people might buy into that philosophy, but she never had. She'd always believed that a person shaped at least part of her destiny. And she couldn't go on avoiding Chase Monroe III forever. She'd just have to learn how to deal with him.

"I'd love to go," she said.

"We'll pick you up in fifteen minutes."

"I LIKE THE BIG SNAKES best," Jason declared as he finally unglued his nose from the glass enclosing a giant boa constrictor.

In Sunny's arms, Emma shivered. "My sentiments exactly, Em. Whenever I see one, my blood runs cold." She lowered the girl to the ground and took her hand.

"I'd like one for a pet," Jason said, clearing a path for them through the crowd in the snake house.

"How would you feed him?" Chase asked. "Their diet consists of small animals. They swallow them whole."

Jason shot a look at Sunny. "You could keep him at your place. You got lots of mice."

Sunny turned and found Chase close. So close that she could catch his scent above the smell of animals and people. His lips were close, too. Another inch or so and they could brush hers. She found it took an effort to move. Away. She did want to move away, didn't she? Warily she met his eyes and saw the glint of . . . what? Understanding? Satisfaction?

"Could I keep him at your house? Could I?"

Sunny glanced down at Jason. "I'm afraid not, honey. Boas eat all kinds of small animals. What if yours gobbled up Gracie?"

Jason sighed in defeat. "All right. I like Gracie. Let's go see the monkeys."

"Just when I was beginning to feel comfortable around the snakes," Chase said.

Once outside, the crowd thinned a little. Sunny began to breathe easier. The sun was warm, enhancing the smells of new-mown grass, animals and popcorn. She steered Jason toward a refreshment cart.

"Large popcorn, no butter," she ordered.

"Make that two," Chase said.

"Ice cream." Jason pointed to a picture displayed on the side of the cart. Emma pointed to a chocolate-covered cone. Then with the children between them, Sunny and Chase strolled down a path that promised to take them to the Monkey House. On one side, reindeer fawns grazed behind a fence. Jason pulled up short at a grain dispenser. "Can we feed the deer?"

Sunny dug into her purse for change and divided it between the children. Jason was the first to fill his hand with grain. Running to the fence, he tossed some of it over.

"No, don't throw it. Hold it, like this." Sunny demonstrated. "They'll come to you."

Following her example, Jason thrust his hand though the wires of the fence and waited, hardly daring to breathe as a fawn approached. Emma pressed herself closer to her brother's side and held out her hand. Taking Sunny's arm, Chase drew her to a nearby bench. For a while they sat in silence as one of the fawns approached Emma. Poised for flight, she managed to stand her ground as the animal nibbled at the grain.

Sunny leaned back against the bench and relaxed for the first time since Chase had picked her up at the carriage house. A baby cried from a passing stroller, and rap music blasted down from the hill above them. Beside her, she could hear Chase chewing his popcorn. Turning her head, she studied him for a minute. His eyes were squinted slightly against the sun as he watched his niece and nephew.

"Somehow that popcorn doesn't fit your image," she said.

He met her eyes. "Why not?"

"It doesn't go with caviar and champagne." But neither did the clothes he was wearing. His jeans were faded and worn, and hugged the lean lines of his body.

Chase shrugged easily. "Maybe you've got the wrong image of me. I told you that stuff was a gift from my mother."

Sunny pictured Lila McIntyre as she appeared in "Gallagher's Dream" and then she thought of the ambitious young actress who'd left her baby to pursue her dream of becoming a star. For the first time she admitted, to herself that she'd misjudged Chase Monroe. It had been easier to think of him as a footloose bachelor with enough money to boost her profit margins. And when she'd found herself attracted to him, it had been safer to try to think of him as a reporter and therefore untrustworthy. But it hadn't been fair.

"I'm sorry."

Chase looked at her in surprise. "Because my mother sent me a birthday present?"

"No. Of course not." She glanced down at her popcorn, picking up a piece and then dropping it back into the box before speaking again. "I read your book."

Chase grinned. "I can understand your being sorry about that. It's pretty dry stuff."

"No. It was good. The picture you painted was so vivid. I was very moved."

He felt a flood of pleasure. It was exactly the effect he wanted his book to have on readers—especially her.

"What made you write it?"

He shrugged. "I was there. I saw how politicians and diplomats can make a monumental problem even worse. So much of the food that was shipped in to feed the hungry just sat on loading docks and spoiled because of arguments over how to distribute it. I thought if the story was told, maybe it wouldn't happen again."

Suddenly, Jason appeared beside the bench. "Do you have any more change?" Setting her popcorn aside, Sunny dug more coins out of her purse. "Share it with Emma," she instructed.

"Has reading my book improved your opinion of reporters?" Chase asked after the little boy had scampered off.

Sunny brushed a piece of popcorn off her lap. "That's what I wanted to apologize for. I judged you based on my previous experience."

"With Jeff Miller." Chase was surprised by the curiosity he was feeling. No, it was more than that. Curiosity didn't burn.

"I dated him for a while just over a year ago," Sunny said. "Right after my uncle was indicted. I should have known when this tall handsome man appeared and asked to do a feature on Service with a Smile that something was up. But I fell for it. When he invited me out to dinner, I even thought he might be interested in me."

"Did you fall in love with him?"

"No. Of course not." She met his eyes squarely. "I don't make a habit of falling in love with men I hardly know."

Only when he heard her denial did Chase become aware of the tension in his shoulders, in his jaw.

"I thought about it, though. That's why I'm still annoyed with myself. Jeff was charming and he knew what kind of wine to order with dinner."

"To loosen your tongue about your uncle."

"You sound as if you're familiar with the technique."

"I've never used it on a woman." Especially an innocent one, he thought.

"Well, it worked," Sunny said. "Uncle Leo agreed to do an exclusive interview because I asked him to. I had no idea that Jeff intended to follow each segment with editorial comments that would turn Uncle Leo's constituency against him."

"Let me get this straight. You blame yourself because your uncle lost his popularity?"

"I blame myself because Uncle Leo went to jail. When everyone turned against him, I'm sure he felt he had to make a deal with the prosecution. If he'd gone to trial, maybe things would have turned out differently."

"Things might have turned out a whole lot worse."

Sunny shook her head. "I know that what Uncle Leo did . . . what he was accused of doing is illegal. But he did a lot of good for this community. For the farmers and for local businesses. Hundreds of people owe their jobs to him. If it hadn't been for those interviews, I think it might have been difficult to find a jury to convict him."

Chase waited for the length of time it took Sunny to toss a kernel of popcorn to three waiting pigeons. He was angry, but not at Sunny. Her loyalty was something he'd admired from the first. "Did it ever occur to you that your uncle got just what he wanted?"

"What do you mean?"

"I've done some research on him. He strikes me as a very astute man. I think he knew exactly what he was doing when he agreed to those interviews. He never wanted his case tried."

"Why not?"

"Because in a plea bargain, both sides have to make concessions. Your uncle wanted something and he got it."

Sunny stared at him for a minute. "You mean money."

"It's a logical assumption."

"But why did he ask me for ten thousand dollars? And why does he want more?"

"You didn't agree?"

"No. I gave him everything I had the first time." Sunny frowned, thinking of his phone call to her mother.

"What is it?"

"Nothing really." The concern in his eyes seemed so genuine that, before she could stop herself, she poured out her worries about her uncle's apparent confusion over the mortgage on her mother's house.

"You're sure he told you he wants the money for an appeal?"

"Yes. He said his lawyers are very hopeful."

It was Chase's turn to frown. "It doesn't make sense. Your uncle's lawyers made a deal with the prosecutors, so there's no verdict that can be appealed."

"Then why...?"

For a moment Chase didn't answer. Blackmail was his first thought, but he knew he had to choose his words carefully. "A lot of people believe those stories about the millions in illegal campaign contributions and payoffs that your uncle has tucked away. Money, especially large amounts of it, can be a powerful motivator."

"Do you think he's in any danger?"

"No." And he was positive about that. Leo Caldwell was a survivor. At all costs. "But he owes you an explanation. When is the next visiting day?"

"This Thursday. I'll ask him then. I'll also tell him about your offer." She met Chase's eyes squarely. "If he accepts, we'll know for sure that he needs the money." This time it was Emma who raced over to them with her hand held out. Sunny was relieved. She needed time to think about what Chase had told her.

"We need more money," Jason shouted from the grain dispenser. Chase dug into his pocket for a handful of coins. "This is all I've got. Make it last." As soon as her fingers closed around the money, Emma spun around and ran back to her brother. Three reindeer fawns waited patiently at the fence.

"Heather believes Emma will start speaking again soon," Sunny said. "How's Jason doing with his thumb?"

"I haven't noticed any change yet. Except for today. I don't think I've seen it in his mouth once."

"It's the zoo. There's so much to see and do."

"It's more than the zoo. They haven't been this relaxed since the last time you were at the apartment and you told them that story about the weightless princess. Heather says you've stopped by several times to check on them."

Sunny shrugged. "I recommended The Growing Place to you. I wanted to make sure they were adjusting."

"You could have called or dropped by my apartment. You're welcome anytime."

She turned to him. "I didn't think that would be wise."

Hadn't he said the same thing to himself each time he'd caught himself reaching for the phone to call her? He lifted one of her curls and wound it around his finger. The sunlight intensified its fiery highlights, yet it was cool to his touch.

Sunny said nothing, but her fingers squeezed tighter on the popcorn box. A few kernels dropped onto her lap.

"Do you always do what's wise?" Chase asked.

"No." She managed a smile. "But I do try to learn from my mistakes."

It was an idea he could relate to, something he prided himself on. Not that he'd allowed himself to make any mistakes where women were concerned. He'd seen his father make too many. Four wives, and not one had made his father happy for any length of time. Always before, Chase had managed to keep his relationships with women enjoyable, but casual. With Sunny, he wasn't at all sure he could do that.

He caught her scent quite clearly above the more pungent animal smells that floated on the cool breeze. She smelled of spring flowers with a hint of spice. "Are you so sure that visiting my apartment would be a mistake?"

"Positive." She brushed the popcorn kernels from her lap. A fat pigeon nudged two others aside for the prize. She glanced at Chase. "I hope you don't take that as some sort of challenge."

He looked at the children, then back at her. "My life is challenging enough right now."

"Yes." She dropped her gaze and turned her attention to feeding the pigeons.

Chase studied her. She was wearing snug jeans, which revealed the slim curves of her hips and legs, and a sweatshirt with a frayed hood. Did she own anything but sweats and jeans? A miniature monkey dangled from one of her ears. Her zoo earrings, she'd explained to Emma.

He could easily understand the children's fascination with her. But for the life of him, he couldn't figure out his own. Sunny Caldwell was not his type. She was so . . . Chase searched for the right word. Involved? Committed?

Whether it was for the sake of her business or the people she cared about, she seemed willing to give one hundred percent of herself. Was that what drew him to her? How could a man keep from wondering what it would be like to make love with a woman like that? And once he had, would it be possible to walk away?

He'd spoken the truth when he'd told her that his life was challenging enough right now. So why had he asked her to come today? For the children? For an interview with her larcenous uncle? Chase wasn't a man who made a habit of lying to himself.

He raised his hand and traced the line of her jaw with his fingers. Her skin was softer than he remembered and cool at first. But he felt the quick warming and his own immediate response to it.

Sunny turned to stare at him, determined to ignore the flash of heat that shot through her and the breathless, weak sensation it left in its wake. She was going to get up and walk away. Just as soon as she could make her legs move.

"Everything you've said makes perfect sense," Chase murmured. "But it doesn't seem to change the fact that I want you."

The blunt statement had her heart hammering in her throat and sent all coherent thought drifting away on the breeze. People continued to stroll by the bench where they were sitting. A child laughed. But Sunny was no longer really aware of anything or anyone except Chase. Good Lord, he had beautiful eyes. The color of smoke that rose quick and hot from a fire. The box of popcorn slipped unnoticed from her hands as she felt the needy, relentless excitement begin to build in the pit of her stomach.

Oh, yes, he definitely wanted her, Chase thought. And it didn't matter a whit that she wasn't his style. Kissing a woman in public wasn't his style either. But that's exactly what he was going to do. Even as he thought of it, his hands, already tangled in her hair, drew her closer. His lips were just touching hers when he saw a blur of movement. Then Sunny jerked away from him.

"My purse!"

Chase spotted a figure in a hooded sweatshirt running up the hill behind them. Chase and Sunny stood up at the same instant, but Chase gripped Sunny's shoulders and pushed her down. "Stay with the kids."

She jumped back up and took several steps in pursuit before his words sank in. Then she whirled around and raced back to the fence.

"C'mon," she said, grabbing Emma and Jason. "We have to catch your uncle."

"Tag?" Jason asked as he tried to pull ahead.

"Sort of," Sunny replied, tightening her grip on his hand.

"Let me go!" Jason said. "Let me catch him."

"No," Sunny said as she steered them out of the way of an oncoming stroller. "We all have to be holding hands when we catch him, or it doesn't count."

"That's dumb," Jason declared. But to Sunny's relief, he stopped trying to free himself. Still, she felt as if she was running last in a three-legged race by the time they made it halfway up the hill. She caught one last glimpse of Chase before he disappeared into the crowd on the path above them. Then Emma stumbled, and Sunny paused to lift her onto one hip. "Wrap your legs around me and hold on tight." Jason jerked them forward.

At the top of the hill, Sunny was panting, and she could feel a trickle of sweat winding its way down her back. There was no sign of Chase or the figure in the hooded sweatshirt.

"Hurry!" Jason wove his way through the lines of people in front of the Monkey House. "Over here."

But when they reached the other side of the path, there was still no sign of Chase.

"Is he hiding?" the little boy demanded.

Sunny couldn't find the breath to answer. Lowering Emma to the ground, she concentrated on getting the air moving in and out of her lungs. Ahead, the path forked. The right side was filled with people on their way to see the new baby elephant. The left one disappeared into the woods. *If I were a thief . . .* With a brief, hopeful prayer she was right, Sunny grabbed Emma's hand and urged both children down the deserted path.

Once they reached the coolness of the trees, the pavement gave way to gravel, deeply indented on either side of a grassy ridge. A service road, Sunny guessed. But the uneven surface slowed them.

"If he's hiding, aren't we supposed to find him?" Jason asked, pulling them along. "I could run ahead. If I see him, I'll come right back."

Sunny crouched down so she could look Jason right in the eye. "You promise you'll only go as far as the bend in the road?"

Jason sketched a cross over his heart. "Promise."

The second she released his hand, he streaked ahead. Lifting Emma into her arms again, Sunny hurried after him.

"I see him! I see him!" Jason jumped up and down, but true to his word, he ran back to grab Sunny's hand and drag her along.

Once they rounded the curve, the path sloped abruptly downward for about a hundred yards and ended at a fence. The man in the hooded sweatshirt had climbed halfway up it, and Chase was pulling him off.

"C'mon, let's tag him!" Jason said.

"No." Sunny held the little boy's hand tightly. "We have to wait until he's through talking to that man."

"Talking?" Jason gave a laugh that sounded like a snort. "He's punching the guy's lights out."

Or vice versa, Sunny thought as the two men rolled over and over on the ground. They were far enough away from the crowds and the animal houses that she could hear the pained grunts and the sound of flesh pounding flesh. Chase was on top, then the other man, then Chase. Finally, locked together, they rolled into a heap against the fence.

Jason tugged at her hand. "Let me go. I gotta help him."

"No," Sunny said, holding fast. But even as she debated her next move, the purse snatcher got away from Chase and launched himself up and over the fence. He'd lost his hood, and she got a clear impression of a slender build and light hair before he dropped to the other side. By the time Chase had reached the top of the fence, the other man had jumped into a car and was racing away.

Sunny and the children hurried down the hill to meet Chase. He was limping, she realized as they drew near.

"You're hurt," she said, dropping to her knees. The faded denim of his jeans bagged over one knee, but it was beginning to fit more snugly around the other.

"I twisted it while we were wrestling. Otherwise, he never would have gotten away. He still has your purse, too."

"Never mind that." She touched his knee gingerly and then pulled her hand back. "It's swelling up quite a bit. You should have it looked at. I'll drive you to the hospital."

"No hospital." His voice was curt.

Rising, Sunny met his eyes squarely. "You should have it x-rayed."

"The same thing used to happen when I played football. I know what to do."

Sunny's brows rose. "Oh? You're a doctor?"

"An ice pack and a couple of aspirin. You can check on me in the morning."

Sunny planted her fists on her hips. "Don't be such a ninny. The hospital is on our way home."

"You're not going to leave us, are you, Uncle Chase?"

They both looked down at Jason. The child's eyes were wide, the fear in them very real.

"No. I don't need a hospital or a doctor," Chase said. He started to squat, then thought better of it. He put his arm around the boy and pulled him close. "Sunny's just a little worried. Right, Sunny?"

She met his eyes and read the message in them loud and clear. "Right." Reaching for Chase's free arm, she settled it on her shoulders, offering as much support as she could. "Let's get your uncle home. You can make the ice pack, Jason. And Emma, you and I will feed him the aspirin."

"*BEAUTY AND THE BEAST!* Why do we have to watch that dumb movie?" Jason grumbled as Sunny showed Emma how to put the tape into the VCR.

Chase dropped his arm around the boy's shoulders. "Now, c'mon. The girls didn't complain during the Ninja Turtle movie, did they?"

"They snuck out to the kitchen during the good part with all the kicking and pounding," Jason complained.

"To clean up," Sunny said as she leaned back against the couch and drew Emma onto her lap. "And we're giving you fair warning. We're not going to play maid all the time. Next time, you guys can wash the dishes."

Chase grinned at Sunny. "Deal. Besides, I prefer it when you play doctor."

Sunny turned her attention quickly back to the TV, but not before she felt the blood rush to her cheeks. He'd needed help getting out of his jeans, and Jason had come rushing out of the bedroom to get her. Between the two of them, they'd managed to work the jeans halfway down his thighs. That was when Sunny's gaze had wandered to the navy briefs he was wearing, and the bones in her fingers had turned to jelly. "Brief" was very definitely the operative word. Not bikini, but close. If it hadn't been for Jason, Chase might have still been stuck half in and half out of his jeans.

Men's underwear wasn't supposed to be sexy, was it? But then Chase Monroe had a way of looking sexy in anything. Especially in nothing at all. The memory made her face grow even hotter. In desperation, she focused her attention on the screen. It wouldn't be long before Belle had her first meeting with the Beast. Lucky girl, Sunny thought. She wouldn't have to deal with a half-naked man.

Chase kept his gaze on the back of Sunny's neck even after the flush had faded. He thought about how little effort it would take to bring that pink color flooding back. Jason stirred against his side, reminding him that Sunny's wouldn't be the only reaction if he followed his inclination and leaned over to kiss her right beneath her ear. Nor would his own response be so easy to hide.

"This is boring," Jason said. "It's just like that story Sunny told to us the other night. The prince will save the princess and they'll live happily ever after."

"Not this time," Sunny said. "In this story, Belle is going to save the Beast."

"From what?" Jason asked. "He's got a neat castle. And look at all that food."

"But he's lonely. Belle will save him from that. See—" Sunny pointed to the the screen "—she's already giving him friendship, and he's starting to think of that drafty old castle as his home."

Chase glanced down at his nephew. The boy didn't look totally convinced. Of course, Jason didn't really understand what loneliness was. And he never would. Chase intended to make very sure of that.

Odd, but he'd never thought of himself as lonely, either. For a long time now, he'd chosen to live alone. And although he'd always enjoyed the process of tracking down a good story, he'd come to prefer the more solitary job of writing it.

Chase turned his attention back to the TV screen. But his mind wasn't on the colorful shapes that flickered across the screen. Instead, he concentrated on what he was feeling. For the first time he could remember, he was sitting in his living room and feeling at home. And it had little to do with the aroma of fried chicken and pizza that still lingered in the air from their fast-food picnic. It had everything to do with the warmth of a small body pressed against his. And for that he could thank the woman who was sitting an arm's length away from him.

A home and children. He'd never allowed himself to think about having those things. Growing up, his life had been lonely, he supposed. Until David had come along. Even when he'd seen David and Laura build something special, he hadn't allowed himself to want the same thing for himself. It had been enough to be a part of their family once or twice a year. His work had always been satisfying.

On the screen a teapot burst into song, and Emma laughed.

Emma? Startled, Chase's brows rose in a question as he met Sunny's eyes. The joy he saw in them confirmed what he thought he'd heard. Emma had laughed. It was the first sound she'd made. On Sunny's face he saw a reflection of his own emotions. Joy. Relief. And something else. The little girl was still sitting on Sunny's lap watching the movie. More than anything he wanted to take them both into his arms. But they weren't to make a fuss when Emma made a sound. Just take it in stride. That had been the advice of the pediatrician.

"Popcorn," Jason announced suddenly, and yawned.

"You can't possibly want any more to eat," Chase said. "You'll get sick."

"I'll get sick, anyway, if there's any kissing in this movie." Jason aimed an accusing look at Sunny. "Is there going to be any of that mushy stuff?"

Sunny laughed and asked, "Will you settle for hot chocolate?" At Jason's nod, she eased Emma off her lap and stood.

"I'll help," Chase offered.

"Your knee—"

"Will be very stiff if I don't walk around." Chase removed the ice pack. "Would you care to examine it more closely, Doctor?"

Sunny's eyes narrowed when she saw the laughter in his. "I'll take your word for it."

He levered himself up from the couch. "Stay with Emma, will you, Jase?"

"Jase?" Sunny asked when they reached the kitchen.

"He asked me to call him that while you and Emma were cleaning up out here."

Sunny smiled at him before she went to the sink to fill the kettle with water. "He wants to be just like his uncle."

"Yeah. I'm not sure how I feel about the responsibility."

"All the really good things in life come with a catch. Children come with a bigger one than usual." She set the kettle over a high flame. When she turned, Chase was blocking her path.

"What can I do to help?" he asked.

"With instant hot chocolate?" she said as she stepped around him and headed for the pantry. "Why don't you sit down and take a load off that knee?" She lifted a box off the lowest shelf. When she turned, she found that he'd followed her.

"My cupboard is no longer bare, I see." He reached over her head to pick up one of the cans.

He'd startled her, Sunny thought. That was why her heart was racing. "Thanks to Aunt Alma. And Service with a Smile, of course." She glanced over her shoulder at the loaded shelves. "I know it looks like a lot of food. But none of it's perishable. It won't go to waste."

Chase placed the can he was holding back on a shelf. "Dinosaur-shaped pasta? I didn't know they made stuff like that."

Ducking under his arm, Sunny walked to the nearest cupboard. She wasn't running away. She couldn't make hot chocolate without cups. "You'd be surprised at what appears on grocery shelves these days specially packaged to appeal to young children." Finding the first cupboard filled with plates, she tried the next one. "I can guarantee most families a twenty-percent savings on their weekly shopping bill by eliminating everything that ends up in their cart simply because their kids are with them." The second door Sunny opened revealed glasses.

"Are you telling me that pasta dinosaurs were on your aunt Alma's list?" Chase asked.

Sunny shot him a guilty look. "Not exactly. Aunt Alma's a very creative cook. Sometimes she gets a little carried away with seasonings. I got the dinosaurs for an emergency. I wouldn't want Jason and Emma to go to bed hungry."

"Of course not. If you're looking for the cups, they're right here." As he reached behind her to open the last cupboard door, his body brushed hers. The contact was brief and surely an accident. Still, Sunny felt the quick rush of heat pulse through her, scattering her thoughts.

"What do we do next?" Chase asked as he lined the cups up on the counter. But his gaze never left Sunny's face.

"Hmm?" Sunny murmured, still not quite coherent.

"Hot chocolate." But he wasn't thinking of making the drink when he reached over to skim his fingers along her cheek and watched her eyes darken. And he knew exactly what he wanted to do next.

Sunny breathed deeply. Her brain needed more oxygen. Then she'd be able to think. And talk. "I... Chase, please..."

"Please what?" He lowered his head to let his lips follow the path his fingers had just taken.

The weakness, the warmth, that flowed through her swept away her words and thoughts until the shrill whistle of the kettle pierced the silence and sent her jerking back into the edge of the counter.

Chase brought his hands to her shoulders to steady her. Her eyes were wide and fixed unblinkingly on his. He saw the confusion and the desire. But it was the trace of fear that had his hands dropping to his sides. "It's mutual, you know. This effect we seem to have on each other."

Sunny drew in another breath. "That doesn't make it right." The kettle's whistle grew more insistent. Sunny moved around Chase, careful not to brush against him. By the time she turned off the burner she felt a little steadier. Still, she was relieved to find he hadn't followed her.

"I think we should finish the conversation we were having before that man snatched my purse," Sunny said.

"As I recall, we weren't talking. I was about to kiss you."

Sunny frowned. "Before that. I told you my coming over here would be a mistake. And apparently I was right."

Now Chase frowned. "Explain the mistake."

"We're attracted to each other. Just where is that going to lead? No." She raised a hand to prevent Chase's reply. "That was a rhetorical question. And the only logical answer is that it can't lead anywhere. Because of those two children in the other room. You're still adjusting to them. And they're adjusting, too. To the loss of their parents and to a new life with you. The last thing you need right now is more complications in your personal life."

"What about you?" Chase asked as he moved the cups to the counter in the center of the kitchen.

"This is a crucial year for my business. I have to devote all my time to developing a wider client base. I don't have time for . . . complications either."

"You make a very compelling argument."

It was relief she was feeling, Sunny told herself as she tore open envelopes and tipped their contents into the cups.

Chase watched her fill four cups with water and begin to stir. She was right. As a writer, he could recognize the value of a well-thought-out argument. But as a reporter, he also knew the importance of instinct. And it was instinct that was telling him he couldn't let Sunny Caldwell walk out of his life. Not when he was just beginning to realize what he wanted from her. Finally he said, "I couldn't agree with you more . . . up to a point. But it's obvious you care very much for Emma and Jase."

She met his eyes. "Yes."

"Then I don't see the need for you to cut yourself off from us entirely. After all, we are adults. We'll just have to do the practical thing and control our feelings."

Before Sunny could say anything, Chase continued, "For the sake of the children. Emma just laughed for the first time. And it has a lot to do with you. When Jason's around you, he seems more like the little boy I used to know. I would hate for either of them to have a setback at this stage. So why don't we agree to take it from here—strictly as pals?"

Sunny said nothing as she stared at the hand he held out to her. He had a logical mind. Hadn't she discovered that when she'd read his book? Why was she hesitating to agree? Did she want to disappoint those children? She took his hand.

"Good. Now that we've cleared the air, I want you to spend the night."

"What?" She jerked her hand out of his grip.

"You can sleep on the couch. Or with one of the kids if you'd feel safer."

"No."

"That man at the zoo stole your purse. Your driver's license was in it, right?"

"Yes."

"Then he has your address. And your keys?"

She nodded.

"I don't want you going back to that carriage house alone tonight. Even if we get the locks changed, he knows your address."

"I'm a big girl. I've been living alone for years."

"Is the hot chocolate ready yet?" Jason and Emma stood in the archway to the kitchen. Jason stuck his thumb into his mouth.

"Don't tell me the movie is over already," Sunny said, waving them over to the counter.

"I paused it."

"Jase, you're just in time to help me convince Sunny to stay overnight with us," Chase said as he lifted Emma onto one of the stools.

"You've got to stay," Jason said as he climbed onto another one. "What if Uncle Chase's knee gets big again in the middle of the night? Who'd tell us what to do?"

Chase grinned at Sunny over the heads of the two children.

"You don't fight fair," Sunny accused.

He lifted his cup to her in a toast. "I do what it takes to get what I want."

5

FROM THE BACK PORCH of The Growing Place, Chase watched Emma put the final touches on a sand castle, then giggle at something Heather's daughter said. The sound carried even above the noisy droning of bees busily attacking the nearby rosebushes. Behind him, Sunny was pacing agitatedly while she cross-examined Heather. It was at Heather's suggestion that they'd brought the children early to the day-care center.

"So what you're saying is that Emma has taken a first step, but the journey's far from over?" Sunny asked.

Heather wrinkled her nose at her friend. "I meant to be more encouraging than that. The fact that she's laughing is a very good sign. But now it's more important than ever to surround her with love and make her feel secure."

"Any specific suggestions?" Chase asked.

"Don't make any sudden changes in her routine."

"She seems most relaxed and happy when Sunny's around," Chase said.

"Then Sunny should continue to spend time with her."

Sunny opened her mouth, but before she could speak, Heather continued, "Any changes at this point could trigger a relapse. And you shouldn't overlook Jason. Just because he hasn't reacted as overtly as Emma has to their parents' deaths doesn't mean he isn't feeling the loss just as deeply."

A small boy burst through the screen door and raced down the steps to join Jason who was perched near the bottom of the jungle gym. Quick as a blink, the boy pulled himself to the very top and was hanging by one hand. A rather harried-looking woman followed in his wake and deposited a sleeping infant in Heather's arms.

"Tell me again that girls are different," the woman pleaded.

"Of course they are," Heather replied in a soothing tone.

The arrival of a pigtailed whirlwind who let out a war whoop on her way to the sandbox gave the lie to Heather's words.

Taking Sunny's arm, Chase steered her through the chaotic flow of arrivals at The Growing Place.

Neither of them spoke until he had parked the car in front of the carriage house. Sunny was already reaching for the door handle when he took her hand in his.

"You're upset because Heather agrees with me that Emma and Jason need you."

"No . . ."

He tightened his grip on her hand when she tried to pull free. "I meant what I said last night. Whatever is happening between you and me, whatever is going to happen, can wait." He released her and rested his arm along the top of the steering wheel.

"Nothing more is going to happen."

He grinned. "Take a tip from a veteran reporter—it's always better to face facts than ignore them."

Sunny glared at him. "Even the best reporters occasionally misinterpret the facts."

She'd forgotten how quickly he could move. Suddenly he was pressing her back against the seat, his mouth almost brushing hers.

"Not this time." Even as he said the words, his lips touched hers, and her own parted in invitation. She hadn't intended them to. And when she placed her hands against his chest, it was to shove him away. But her hands betrayed her, her fingers curling into his shirt and pulling him closer. She could feel the response flow out of her as her tongue met his. Then her arms were around him before she was aware that they'd moved.

Dazed, Chase took what she offered. He knew he should pull away, think. Hadn't he meant to reassure her that this wouldn't happen again? But her response poured into him, igniting a flame that set off a thousand little explosions of need. So he drew her closer to absorb just a little more of her softness, her strength. Would he ever get enough?

When Chase finally pulled away, he had to wait for a moment for his head to clear. Kissing her was not part of his plan. But then, from the very beginning, he hadn't been able to come up with much of a plan for dealing with his feelings for Sunny. He took a deep breath and found some comfort in the fact that she looked just as shaken as he was. Her eyes were wide and clouded with desire. He put all his effort into concentrating on the point he'd been trying to make.

"We *are* going to make love," he said. "But for now, my priority is the children." He leaned back against the door. "They both need you. You saw Jason this morning, just sitting there on that jungle gym. It's only when he's around you that he's anything like he used to be. Mischievous, playful. And I want you to feel comfortable around them. So for the time being, let's be friends."

"Friends?" Sunny was surprised that her lips had formed the word, that her breath had produced the sound. "We'd better define *friends*."

"Be my guest."

Sunny tried to think. "Any time we spend together will be with the children." She paused, frowning. Hadn't they been doing that already? And it hadn't helped. "No romantic situations."

His eyebrows rose. "Are you going to define that, too?"

"You know what I mean." Seeing the laughter in his eyes, she narrowed her own slightly. "Absolutely *no* kissing."

"Agreed."

It occurred to her he'd agreed rather easily. Still, as she opened the door and climbed out of the car, she congratulated herself on laying the ground rules. Crossing to one of the terra-cotta urns that flanked the door of the carriage house, she fished her spare key from beneath one of the plants.

"As a *friend*, I'd like to point out that that's a very obvious hiding place."

"This is a very safe neighborhood. Some people even leave their doors unlocked," Sunny said as she opened the door.

Two steps into the room, she stopped short, and Chase had to sidestep quickly to keep from walking into her. The place looked as though a tornado had whipped through it. On the long tables that lined the walls, boxes had been overturned, their contents tossed willy-nilly across the floor. Here and there manila folders sat steepled over the debris like markers in a graveyard.

Speechless, Chase stared at the senseless destruction, then at Sunny. Her face was pale, her body rigid.

He reached out and pulled her close, hoping to comfort her, while the bitter taste of rage rose in his throat. Swallowing, he pushed it back, vowing to let it out when the time was right. When he discovered who had done this.

Much harder to deal with was the frustration he felt. What could he possibly do to comfort Sunny? What could he say? He could only imagine what it felt like to come home and find his apartment violated, the pages of his manuscript strewn across the floor.

Searching for words, he ran his hand softly over her hair and heard her breath go out on a sigh as she wrapped her arms around him. Suddenly, beneath his anger, he felt a wave of warmth and softness. Always before when he'd held her, there'd been fire, an explosion of excitement and desire. But that wasn't what he was feeling now. It occurred to him he could hold her this way for hours and be happy.

When she'd closed her eyes and leaned against him, Sunny had promised herself it would only be for a minute. She was so cold, but she was determined not to shiver. When he'd held her before, she'd found heat. But this time it was different. Instead of fire weakening her, she felt warmth, solid and sure. There was strength here, too. She could hear it in the steady beat of his heart. For one more minute she would allow herself to draw on it. How long had it been since she'd relied on anyone's strength but her own? It was that thought that inflated the little bubble of panic in her stomach and had her drawing away.

Then she dropped to her knees and began to pick up the papers.

"I don't think we should touch anything until the police get here," Chase said.

"Police?" Sunny looked around the room again. "Of course." Rising, she walked into the kitchen.

While she punched in the number, Chase inspected the front door. Then he joined her and filled two glasses with cola.

Coffee would have been better, he thought, preferably laced with brandy. It might have brought the color back to her cheeks. Still, he was relieved to see that her hand was steady when she lifted the glass and drained its contents.

"The door hasn't been forced. Who else has a key?" he asked when she was finished.

"Hector. And of course, Aunt Marnie and Aunt Alma keep a spare at the house. But none of them would do this."

"That leaves our friend from the zoo."

"But why?"

"He could have been looking for money, jewelry."

Sunny swept her gaze around the room. "In my files?"

"What do you keep in those boxes?"

"Customer addresses, weekly orders. We store them for a few months in case there's a complaint."

"What about tax records, insurance, payroll?"

Sunny waved a hand. "Some of it's on the computer. Hector handles all of it for me."

"Does your uncle Leo know that Hector has most of your records on the computer?"

"You can't possibly think that Uncle Leo had anything to do with this. He's in jail!"

Chase set his glass down. "He has friends."

Sunny shook her head.

"Enemies."

Her frown deepened into a scowl. "Why?"

"That's something I want to ask Leo in person. I'm coming with you the next time you visit him."

"No."

"There's no way I'm going to let you drive to that prison alone. Not after your purse was snatched." He waved a hand at the room. "Not until we find out who's behind this."

Sunny turned to survey the damage once more and clasped her hands together tightly. Papers covered almost every inch of the floor—order blanks, copies of all the original paperwork and loan forms she'd kept on file in hopes of eventually franchising her business. She didn't want to think about how much time it would take to put everything back in order. Halfway down the room, a few scattered papers shifted and settled.

"Look." She pointed. "Those papers just moved." She hurried toward them.

"It may be a mouse," Chase warned.

"We can't let it smother." But when she lifted the papers, it was Gracie she found, lying very still.

Chase grabbed her hands before she could touch the bird. "Better not. Do you have a vet?"

"Her number's by the phone," Sunny said.

"Dios mio!" Hector paused in the open doorway and stared. Then he kept up a steady stream of Spanish as he took in the damage and walked over to Sunny.

She glanced up at him when she felt his fingers close over her shoulder. "Her heart's beating. Look."

The moment he got off the phone, Chase joined them.

"What can I do?" Hector asked.

"See what's missing," Chase replied. "Sunny says you keep track of all the important records. Mortgage, insurance." He followed Hector to the computer and watched as the monitor came to life.

"Don't tell me Gracie did this!"

Chase turned to see a tall woman in running tights step through the door. She carried a small black bag in her hand. "I'm Nancy Ann Tummino." She flashed him a smile as she knelt and began to gently examine Gracie. "Neighborhood vet."

"How did you—"

"Get here so fast? I ran. But only from two doors down." Carefully lifting Gracie, she carried her to the counter in the kitchen with Sunny and Chase close behind.

"Will she be all right?" Sunny asked.

Nancy Ann removed a stethoscope from her bag and hooked it in her ears. After a moment she said, "Her heartbeat's strong. And there don't seem to be any external injuries."

"She moved," Sunny said. "Just a few minutes ago. That's how we found her."

Nancy Ann smiled. "A good sign. Do you know how long she's been like this?"

Sunny shook her head.

"Excuse me."

They all turned to see a uniformed officer at the door. He glanced down at his notebook. "Ms. Caldwell?"

When Sunny started toward him, she found her fingers linked with Chase's. "Stay with Gracie," she said as she let go.

As soon as she was out of earshot, Chase turned to Nancy Ann. "Will the bird recover?"

"I want to take her into the clinic for X rays. And then I'll observe her for a few days. But it looks to me like she flew into a window or the wall and knocked herself out.

It happens more often than you might think. If that's the case, she should be fine."

"Do whatever you need to. Money won't be a problem."

Nancy Ann studied him for a moment and then slowly smiled. "No, it won't. Sunny has an unlimited line of credit with me."

"Oh?"

Before I met her, I used to spend Saturday mornings grocery shopping with my kids. A fate, well, not worse than death, but close. Now she buys groceries for me, and on Saturdays, I coach soccer for my kids' team. And of course, she told me about The Growing Place." She paused before asking, "Are you a friend of hers?"

"Yes."

"Good. She needs someone to look out for her. Takes too much on her shoulders if you ask me." She packed her stethoscope back in the bag. "Can you find me a box?"

Chase pulled one out of a drawer, but it was filled with coupons. He was about to dump them out when Nancy Ann said, "No. She spends hours getting those in order. And that's a good example of why she needs a friend. She clips thousands of coupons to save her customers money." Pulling open another drawer, she located an empty box and settled Gracie into it. "'Course when she saves them money, she cuts down on her profit, too, since she charges a percentage of the total."

Chase looked over at the couch where Sunny was talking to the policeman. A woman of contrasts, he thought. Hadn't that been one of the things that had attracted him from the beginning? A businesswoman who presented herself as totally focused on becoming a millionaire, but who carried her oldest customers on her own credit card and clipped coupons to save them money.

Nancy Ann stopped to let Sunny say goodbye to the bird on her way out. While the farewells were in progress, Chase carefully made his way over to Hector, who was frowning at his computer screen.

"Find anything?"

"Whoever it was turned the computer on." Hector pointed to a flashing number on the screen. "See. It recorded the time—3:48 a.m." He flashed Chase a grin. "I'm dedicated to Service with a Smile, but at that time of the morning, I'm in bed."

"Do you lock your files?"

"Absolutely. And the password is always in Spanish. So I figure he didn't get in. Nothing's missing that I can see."

"How about the original records?" Chase asked.

Hector pointed to the end of the table. "The box is usually right there." He and Chase glanced around the room at the scattered papers. "Now they could be anywhere."

"So the burglar could have found them?"

Hector nodded. "But why would a thief want information, instead of cash?"

"If my theory is correct, money is the final object."

"Why do you—" Suddenly Hector grinned. "Uh-oh, here come Sunny's guardian angels. I'd better help with the wheelchair."

Chase turned to see Alma Caldwell barrel into the room. "What in the world . . . ?"

"What is it?" called a voice from outside.

"A mess! That's what it is!" declared Alma, throwing up her hands. Then she turned to the policeman who was just closing his notebook. "I'll need help with the wheelchair." Taking him by the arm, she hurried him out the door. Hector followed.

Chase started toward Sunny, and she met him in the center of the room. "What did the police say?" he asked.

"They'll file a report and assign a patrol car to swing by a few times during the night.

"What about checking for fingerprints?"

Sunny's eyebrows shot up. "We're not exactly dealing with a major crime here. We're not even sure anything's missing."

When Chase's expression darkened and he moved toward the door, Sunny grabbed his arm. "Look, I just calmed myself down. Don't make me nervous again."

Chase felt the frustration roll through him as her smile formed and then wavered. He wanted her nervous. But he wanted her calm and secure at the same time. "Sunny, I—"

He was interrupted by a voice from behind him.

"You must be Chase."

He turned to find a white-haired lady in a wheelchair smiling up at him. "I'm Sunny's aunt Marnie."

Chase took her hand and lifted it to his lips.

"Oh, my," Marnie said. "You're even better than I thought you'd be."

"I am?"

Sunny took his arm and guided him toward the door. In a low voice she said, "Don't ask her what she means. Unless you have a week free."

Alma waylaid them in the doorway. "Nice to see you, Mr. Monroe. This one needs someone to watch over her. Here," she said, thrusting a tray of mugs at them. "Have some tea. It'll soothe your nerves."

"Thanks," Chase said, grabbing one as Sunny muttered under her breath and hauled him ruthlessly out to the yard.

"You may find Aunt Alma's tea unusual," Sunny warned.

At the car, Chase turned to her. "Let me guess. You're trying to get rid of me."

Sunny grinned. "I always knew you reporters were bright."

He glanced back at the carriage house. "I hate to—"

"Leave me alone?" she asked. "I've got Hector and my aunts to protect me. Aunt Alma's tea alone would be enough to scare most intruders away." Taking the mug from him, she emptied it onto the driveway. "And you've got a book to write and a TV station to check on."

"I don't want you sleeping here tonight."

"That's nonsense."

"Is it?" He placed his hands on her shoulders and barely kept himself from giving her a shake. "Don't argue with me on this. I don't want you to end up like Gracie." Even as he said the words, he pictured in his mind exactly how Sunny would have looked lying still and lifeless on the floor of the carriage house. Pulling her against him, he kissed her.

The contact was brief. Still, Sunny had no trouble sensing his frustration. And she had no trouble feeling his desire. Should she have guessed how much she wanted this? Needed this?

Suddenly Chase pushed her away. Swearing under his breath, he dropped his hands to his sides. "I'm sorry. I didn't mean to break the rules." He held up a hand. "No, let me finish. I meant what I said earlier. We'll be friends. But I want you to stay with me and the children until we find out who did this and why."

Friends, Sunny thought as she stared at him. She could still feel the desire uncoiling inside her, and he was only looking at her.

"I promise," Chase said. "It'll be good for the children, too. So will you come?"

Sunny remembered how Gracie had looked, and she nodded. The prudent thing would be to move in with Chase and the children.

Then as she watched him back out of the driveway, she called herself a liar.

6

WITH A FROWN Sunny aimed the remote control at the TV and zapped the image on the screen out of existence. What was television coming to, anyway? Who in the world wanted to watch a reality-based cop show? With no shoot-outs, no car chases. The police didn't catch the bad guys. They weren't even sure who the bad guys were!

With a disgusted sigh, she began to wander around the room. Didn't she have enough uncertainty in her life without having to watch it on television? No wonder her aunts preferred soap operas. At least there was a storyline and some possibility of a happy ending. When she realized the direction her thoughts had led, she stopped dead in her tracks.

Was she feeling uncertain about her life? Surely not. Besides, the only happy ending she wanted had to do with franchising Service with a Smile.

Turning, she paced in a wide circle around the couch. She was just worried about visiting her uncle tomorrow. If only Chase wasn't going with her. But he had found a solution to every objection she'd made. The children were going to stay at Heather's for dinner in case they were delayed. He'd even managed to get through to Uncle Leo's attorneys and arrange to have his name put on the visitors' list.

Taking a deep breath, she stopped in front of the bookcase. Nothing bad was going to happen tomorrow. Uncle Leo could decide for himself if he wanted to do the interview. And of course, he would explain that he had nothing whatsoever to do with the break-in. Then she could move back into the carriage house and concentrate on business again.

She found herself staring at the model airplane that stood alone on the third shelf of the bookcase. Jason and Chase had been working on it steadily for the past three nights. They would sit at the counter in the kitchen, their heads close together, patiently fiddling with glue and tiny pieces of plastic while she and Emma read stories. Her lips curved as she thought about it. Sweet. But the smile faded from her face as she walked back to the couch. She really was going to miss the children.

And Chase? She'd promised herself she was not going to think about him. In the three nights she'd been sleeping on his couch, he had not spent even one minute with her unless Emma and Jason were also present. The moment the children were in bed, he would disappear into his room to work on his book. He'd kept his word, and that was fine with her!

Lifting a pillow, she began to punch it into shape. And for just an instant she caught his scent. More subtle, more unique than something from a bottle, it had her whirling to see if he was in the room. But he wasn't. She threw the pillow back on the couch. She was doing it again. Thinking about Chase Monroe. Restless, she wandered down the hall to check on Jason and Emma.

Chase counted each one of her footsteps as he stared at his blank computer screen. He hadn't written more than a few pages since she'd started staying in the apartment. And it looked as though he was going to get even less done tonight. He looked at the pile of notes on his desk. The research for the next chapter was complete. And the outline had given him no problems. Rising, he walked to the window. The last time he'd looked out, the sky had still been holding on to a pale light. Now the darkness had conquered, and the lights of the city fanned out below him.

But it was Sunny who was on his mind. All week long she'd been interfering with his concentration, slipping into his thoughts and tangling them up. No other woman had ever affected his work before.

The sound of her footsteps moving past his door again had him clenching his hands. He wanted her. He'd known that much for quite a while. And he knew the desire was mutual, simmering beneath the surface every minute they spent together with the children. He'd given her his word, and he'd kept it. But it had cost him far more than he'd imagined.

What was it about her? That was the question he'd been asking since the first time he'd found her standing in the doorway of his apartment. Tonight he intended to begin finding the answer. Before a problem could be solved, it had to be faced. That had always been the underlying purpose of his writing.

The moment the doorbell rang, he hurried out of his room.

"Hector," Chase said as he opened the door. "You're right on time."

"I brought along a surprise," Hector said, handing a bird cage to Chase.

"Gracie?" Sunny asked, hurrying down the hall. "I thought she had to stay at the clinic until Saturday."

"Dr. Tummino dropped her by the carriage house tonight while I was working on the computer. Says Gracie will convalesce better at home. But if you ask me, it's because the doc's tired of listening to Gracie's . . . complaints."

"There's a diaper pin on the cage door," Sunny said.

Hector grinned. "The latest in vet technology. Seems our little Gracie got loose at the clinic, in spite of the new cage." After handing a linen-covered picnic basket to Chase, he began to back toward the elevator. "She picked up some new words, too, practiced them every time the van hit a bump on the way over here. I'm not responsible for anything she says in English."

"Can't you stay to help us celebrate?" Chase asked.

"I have another delivery. Mrs. Barnstable, my last Wednesday-night customer. She bakes a mean apple pie."

"Celebrate?" Sunny asked as Chase closed the door.

"Gracie's homecoming." He led the way to the kitchen and began to unpack the basket. "Pâté, some French brie and champagne."

"Pâté? Where did you . . . ?" Hurriedly settling Gracie's cage on the counter, she picked up one of the neatly wrapped packages and inspected the label. Her eyes widened. "You sent Hector to Mimi's Gourmet Shop?"

Chase popped the champagne cork. "He suggested it."

"I'll bet he did. The ten percent he collected on this order is more than we get from many of our weekly customers." She took the glass he handed her and sipped. The icy dry taste tempted her to take a second swallow. "Very nice."

He spread pâté on a cracker and handed it to her. "It occurred to me that between your business and my niece and nephew, you haven't had much time to practice your visualization techniques."

She took a bite and closed her eyes as she chewed and swallowed. "It reminds me of liverwurst," she said, wrinkling her nose.

Chase grinned. "There's no arguing with a discriminating palate."

"Maybe Gracie will like it." She shoved the rest of her cracker between the bars of the cage, and they watched as Gracie pecked at the pâté, then returned to her perch.

"That makes it unanimous," Chase said. "Have another sip of champagne before you try the brie." Then he watched as she tasted the cheese. Was she aware that a tiny line appeared on her forehead when she concentrated on something? And that he had a compelling urge to reach out and smooth it away? He took a quick swallow of his wine. But the flavor only made him think of Sunny's taste.

"It's very creamy and smooth," she said as she set the rest of her cracker down.

"It's bland, and you're disappointed."

"No. But some experiences have more inspirational value than others."

"I couldn't agree more."

"I'm talking about the champagne." She raised her glass. "It's very different than the one we tasted the other night."

He turned the bottle so that she could read the label. "Many people believe it's the best champagne in the world. It was first made by a Dominican monk named Dom Perignon."

She took another sip and smiled. "Yes, this will do nicely as a motivator. I bet I'll have to haul a lot of grocery bags to buy it."

"Not if you get your customers to shop at Mimi's Gourmet Shop," Chase said as he poked a piece of brie into Gracie's cage.

The bird immediately dropped from her perch. "What the hell! What the hell!"

Chase and Sunny looked at each other and laughed.

"No wonder Nancy Ann decided to spring her early," Sunny said.

"First I corrupted my nephew and now your bird. Of course it's the dream of every writer to have his words immortalized. But I would have preferred something else."

Sunny rested her elbows on the counter and studied Chase. "You think of yourself as a writer now."

He tipped more champagne into their glasses. "I suppose I do."

"Was it hard to give up reporting?"

"Not really. I got tired of living out of suitcases, hunting down facts." He pulled his glass toward him. "At some point I decided that the only thing I really liked about my life was the writing. And books are a little more permanent than newspapers. Less likely to end up in the trash at the end of the day."

Sunny smiled. "You haven't lost your cynical edge. And you haven't really given up the media entirely."

Chase grimaced. "The TV station. I did that as a favor for an old friend. Dave Yancey. The deal was that I would just put up the money and be a silent partner. But when the symphony went bankrupt, I agreed to do a few editorial commentaries. And I couldn't say no when Dave asked me to fill in after Jeff Miller took that job in Chicago."

Chase watched Sunny over the rim of his wineglass. She was relaxed, comfortable, with her elbows resting on the counter across from him. The mention of Jeff Miller's name hadn't changed that.

Sunny reached for her glass and turned the stem between her fingers. "I thought about what you said at the zoo, about Uncle Leo knowing exactly what he was doing when he agreed to those interviews. You could be right." She looked up at him. "I still hate it that Uncle Leo's in prison. But I don't feel quite so guilty anymore. Thanks."

"You're welcome." She was easy to talk to. Why hadn't he noticed that before? "What about you? Why did you decide to open a grocery-shopping business?"

"Because everybody needs groceries. Think about it. It doesn't matter whether you're rich or poor, young or old. You have to eat. And for most people, that means going to the grocery store. The market is huge."

Listening to her as she warmed to her subject, he could almost feel her energy, her enthusiasm. What would happen, he wondered, if she focused all that on a man?

She waved a hand. "Of course I did a lot of research first. I didn't inherit my father's knack for inventing things. So it made sense to choose a service as my product."

"And you enjoy grocery shopping?"

"I absolutely loathe it. I hated it from the first day I started doing it for my mother. But she was terrible at it. Whenever she did the shopping, we'd have plenty of cookies and candy at the beginning of the week, but by the end, we'd be out of the essential things like milk and bread."

"Candy and cookies aren't a problem for you?"

Sunny grinned. "I didn't say that. I just don't go down those aisles."

"I see. You deal with temptation by avoiding it."

Sunny gave him a level look. "It works for me." Until now, she thought. But then she wasn't avoiding it. Here she was drinking champagne with the very man who'd kissed her senseless less than a week ago. Suddenly her throat went dry. But when she raised her glass, he wrapped his hand around hers to steady it while he topped off the champagne.

They each felt the acceleration of her pulse.

"Odd," Chase murmured. "It hasn't been working for me at all. Right now I want to touch you." His glance lowered to her throat for a moment. "Right where your pulse is beating so fast. And I want to kiss you there, too. And taste your skin as it warms." His eyes returned to hers. "And more. Spending the past three nights alone in my room hasn't made the wanting go away."

As he said the words, Sunny could picture very clearly what it would be like. How his hands would feel on her skin. What she would feel. She was aware of the coolness of the champagne on her wrist before she realized her hand was shaking. Quickly she set the glass down.

"Some things are meant to be, Sunny."

For a moment, she said nothing. Then she pushed herself off the stool and away from the counter. "No.

We agreed not to be together except with the children. If we just stick to that, then..." She made it halfway out of the kitchen before she turned. "We discussed all of this before. We are not going to...whatever it is you have in mind."

"*Que sera, sera,*" Gracie said.

Ridiculous, Sunny thought as she reached the safety of the living room. What did a bird know?

In the kitchen, Chase sat for a long time. Until the champagne was gone. He was sure the bird had it right.

SUNNY STARED out the window at the passing scenery. At times the trees pressed close to the car, their branches forming a canopy of leaves overhead. Then quite suddenly, the trees would give way to open fields crisscrossed by fences. Every so often she could catch the scent of manure and freshly turned earth.

So far, the five-hour drive had passed in relative silence. They had begun the day arguing over whose car they would take. Chase had won only because he happened to have a full tank of gas, and she hadn't wanted to disturb the children who were still half-asleep when they'd dropped them off at The Growing Place.

Actually, she should be looking forward to the meeting with her uncle. He would confirm that the break-in at the carriage house had had nothing to do with him, and then she could move back into her home. Surely with a little distance between them, she and Chase could manage to control their...what? Physical attraction?

Chase saw Sunny's determined nod out of the corner of his eye. Even without asking, he knew exactly what she was thinking. Or plotting. A quick escape from their present living arrangements. Easing his foot off the gas pedal, he let the car sail through an intricate turn.

During the long, restless night, he'd tried to analyze exactly what he felt for Sunny. He'd been attracted to women before, but the attraction had never made him impulsive. Or irrational. Those were things that were supposed to occur only when a person fell in love. Chase frowned as he once again pressed his foot on the accelerator. He certainly wasn't in love, was he?

He was grateful to her. And concerned about her safety. And tremendously attracted to her. Did that add up to love?

"You're going to take a right at the next intersection," Sunny said, straightening in her seat.

As Chase negotiated the turn, the federal correctional facility came into view. The cluster of brick buildings surrounded by well-kept lawns looked more like the campus of a community college than a prison. But once Sunny had directed him to a parking lot and they had joined other visitors in the administration building, the differences were quite apparent. A guard checked their identification and crossed their names off an approved list. Then they were directed to walk through a metal detector and eventually led through a maze of corridors to a large room filled with tables.

A cafeteria, Chase decided when he saw the vending machines lining one of the walls. There were guards at the doors and two who walked up and down between the tables where inmates sat, some by themselves and others already greeting visitors. Sunny scanned the room and then led the way to a far corner.

"Let me do the talking," she whispered.

Her uncle stood when he saw her. Sunny leaned across the table to give him a quick hug.

"I've brought a friend," she said.

"So I see."

Chase met Leo's eyes above Sunny's head and studied him carefully. Gone were the trademark silk shirts and the one-of-a-kind suits. But even in regulation prison garb, Leo Caldwell still managed to look senatorial. Chase's gaze wandered from the older man's perfectly styled white hair to the hand that still held Sunny's. At least there was one thing they agreed on. Sunny needed to be protected.

"Uncle Leo, this is Chase Monroe."

Leo did not extend his hand, and neither did Chase. Leo's eyes were cool and assessing. "My attorneys told me you had an offer to present, Mr. Monroe. But I don't give interviews."

Sunny patted her uncle's arm. "He's willing to reimburse you for your time. Quite generously. And I know you can use the money. I think you should at least hear him out."

Leo turned to her. "Where did you get the idea that I need money?"

"From your phone call. The other night."

Leo glanced at Chase and then back at Sunny again. "I didn't call you."

"Did you call Sunny's mother in Florida?" Chase asked.

Leo shook his head slowly.

"Someone called both Sunny and your sister-in-law, identifying himself as you and asking for money."

"You sounded desperate," Sunny added. "Not like yourself at all."

"He also inquired about insurance policies and the possibility of borrowing against the mortgage on your sister-in-law's house." Chase moved toward the table. "The carriage house on your property was burglarized, too. Nothing was taken, but a pretty thorough search was made of all Sunny's records." He could see he had Leo's full attention, so he turned to Sunny. "It might be easier if your uncle and I talked about this privately."

"Don't be ridiculous," Sunny said.

Leo looked thoughtfully at his niece. "I've changed my mind, Sunny. I might be very interested in Mr. Monroe's offer. Why don't you wait outside?"

Sunny looked from one man to the other, opened her mouth and then shut it. Finally she gave her uncle a quick hug. "Love you."

Leo squeezed her hand before he released her. "I love you, too."

Only after Sunny left the room did the two men sit down across from each other.

"What's your interest in all of this, Mr. Monroe?" Leo asked.

"I want to protect Sunny."

CHASE WAS FROWNING when the prison doors finally slammed shut behind him. There was only one thing he was sure of. Leo Caldwell cared about his niece. But in spite of that, he'd put her in danger. The anger Chase had managed to control for the past half hour threatened to boil up again.

He spotted Sunny pacing in front of his car. How much should he tell her? And how much would she believe about her beloved uncle?

The moment she saw him, she ran to meet him. "What did he tell you?"

Chase hesitated, searching for the right words.

Sunny grabbed the lapels of his jacket. "Tell me. I only left because I knew he wouldn't talk in front of me."

"You're not going to like it," Chase warned.

"I don't much like it that he's in jail for ten years. But I can only help him if I know what's going on."

"Help *him?* You're the one who's in danger."

Sunny gave his lapels a quick jerk. "He would never—"

"Hurt you?" Chase interrupted. "Not intentionally. But he's being blackmailed, and he convinced the blackmailer you're his only source of income."

"Good grief," Sunny murmured, then realized she was still clutching his jacket. Dropping her hands, she took a quick step away. "Who's blackmailing him? And why?"

"Arnie Zimmerman." Steering her around the car, he opened the passenger-side door and walked back to the driver's side. "He wants money."

Frowning at him over the top of the car, Sunny asked, "Who is Arnie Zimmerman?"

"A friend from the old days. Seems Arnie did a few jobs for your uncle when he first went to Albany."

"What kind of jobs?" She marched around the car until she was standing toe-to-toe with him. "And leave off the sugarcoating. If I'm going to help Uncle Leo, I need all the gory details."

"You want details? Okay. Fine. Maybe it's time you had them. Arnie Zimmerman is an arsonist. About twenty years ago he torched a whole block of con-

demned buildings for some of your uncle's supporters."

"Was anyone hurt?"

Seeing the quick leap of panic in her eyes, Chase re-
lented a little. "No. I suppose we should be grateful for
small favors. According to Leo, Arnie was very careful. He always checked the premises before he set a fire
to make sure he wouldn't accidentally barbecue some
unsuspecting tramp."

"You're angry," Sunny said.

"Yes."

"I just want to help Uncle Leo get out of this mess."

"There's a vital fact you seem to be missing here." He
leaned toward her. "Your uncle is not the one who needs
help. He's safely locked up with security checks and
armed guards to protect him. You, on the other hand,
have had your purse stolen, your place of business ransacked and your bird knocked out cold."

"All the more reason we have to do something about
this Arnie Zimmerman."

Chase drew in a deep breath and let it out. "I might
have known you'd find a way to make solving Leo
Caldwell's problems seem logical." He saw hope spring
to life in her eyes and knew he was lost. "Get in the car.
If we're going to talk about this, I need coffee."

For the first few miles, they drove in silence. Sunny
stared straight ahead, too worried to even notice the
passing scenery.

Finally, turning to Chase, she said, "There's still one
thing I'm not clear about. What exactly is this Arnie
Zimmerman blackmailing my uncle about?"

Braking, Chase pulled into the graveled parking lot
of a roadside diner. "It's about money. Oh, there are the

minor matters of insurance fraud and arson. But for your uncle, the bottom line is always money. And he made quite a bundle on that little bonfire of Arnie's. If the feds get wind of it, they might start to sniff around some of his other investments over the years. Not that Leo's apologizing for any of it, you understand. He prefers to view burning that block of buildings as a public service. He told me that within a year, the area became the site for a new subsidized-housing project. No doubt he had his finger in that pie, too. The only things he seems to regret are placing you in danger and making the mistake of believing that five thousand dollars would buy Arnie's silence."

"Five thousand? I lent my uncle ten thousand."

"Taking kickbacks is a hard habit to break."

"I see."

Before she glanced away, he saw the confusion in her eyes change to hurt. Did she have any idea how much he wanted to strangle her uncle? Or how much he wanted to take her in his arms and hold her? His hands tightened into fists. If he touched her now . . . Feeling helpless, he said, "How about some coffee?"

"Coffee would be good." As she fumbled with the door handle, she tried to recall how many times she'd defended her uncle since his arrest. What could she possibly say to make Chase understand? By the time she got out of the car, he was there, waiting. Straightening her shoulders, she said, "He'll pay me back."

"That's one thing we agree on."

He was frowning. His eyes revealed nothing but anger. Carefully she folded her hands together in front of her and searched for the right words. "I don't expect you to understand. I know that, in your eyes, in most people's eyes, my uncle is nothing but a crook. But he's always taken care of my family. After my dad died, he was like a father to me, and . . . I love him."

Jealousy. Should he have known that it could burn and slice so close to the bone? Wasn't her loyalty something he admired about her? He should have realized it was inextricably bound up with her love.

"I don't want Uncle Leo hurt by this. We'll just have to find Mr. Zimmerman and—" she lifted her hands and then dropped them "—explain that I don't have any money."

Chase grabbed her by the shoulders. "Dammit, Sunny. Haven't you figured it out yet? The man sets fires. My guess is he's planning to burn the carriage house. Leo told me he took out a healthy policy on it years ago."

Sunny stared at Chase while her mind raced, reviewing the facts. She thought of the static-filled phone call, the mention of insurance, the files strewn all over the floor of the carriage house. "The guy must have seen the policy."

"Exactly."

"What about my mom's house? My aunts—"

"Leo says Arnie won't bother with the house. Only your mom could collect on that policy. But your uncle would collect if the carriage house burns down."

"Uncle Leo would never agree to this!"

"No," Chase said. "But it's his opinion this is what Arnie plans to do."

Frowning, Sunny said, "We'll have to stop him."

"The police will do that."

"No. Arnie'll tell them what he knows about Uncle Leo. We have to find him, convince him that Uncle Leo will give him the money. Will you help me?"

"Sunny..." He let out his breath in frustration. "Our priorities are very different. You want to protect your uncle. I want to protect *you*."

"Well, maybe we can both get what we want," she said.

"Yeah." What he wanted right now was to shake her. But his hands moved with a will of their own from her shoulders down to her waist and pulled her close. "Maybe we can."

Once his mouth touched hers, he was lost. His anger melted the moment he felt the softness of her lips. Then he couldn't seem to get close enough. The sensations ripping through him were familiar, yet different somehow. Desire cut more sharply, deeply. Even her taste was stronger, tart and sweet at the same time. A flavor he would always crave. He hadn't meant to touch her. Hadn't he promised her he wouldn't? Not until she was safe. But he couldn't seem to stop himself. One hand pressed her closer. The other lost itself in the silky softness of her hair. Holding her this way, it was so easy to believe she was everything he would ever want.

A pickup truck pulled into the lot where they were standing, scattering gravel. Neither of them paid attention to it, nor the long, low whistle of the driver as he strolled slowly into the diner.

It was just as she'd remembered and dreamed about, Sunny thought as she framed his face with her hands and threaded her fingers through his hair. Here was the fire, the rush of heat through her veins, the giddiness, as if she was suddenly caught up in a whirlwind.

Then the quick nip of his teeth on her lower lip made it suddenly all new and unique. So different. Always before when he'd kissed her, her instinct had been to run. This time all she wanted to do was reach out and take more. Only with Chase was the pleasure this intense, the desire this desperate.

A truck roared by on the highway, so close that the wind it left in its wake forced them back against the car.

When Chase drew away, Sunny stood where she was, using the car for support. Another truck raced by. The rush of wind chilled her skin, making her even more aware of the searing heat she'd felt only seconds before.

Chase shook his head to clear it. She truly did want him as much as he wanted her. The joy of it was almost as dizzying as the kiss. He stuffed his hands into his pockets. If he touched her again . . . She was about to speak when he said, "How about that cup of coffee?"

Sunny inhaled deeply and wished it was as easy to gather together her scattered thoughts. "You know, I don't think we should call the police about Arnie."

Chase threw back his head and laughed. "Your uncle made the same suggestion. He advised me to hire a security firm to stake out the carriage house and nab Mr. Zimmerman."

"That's a great idea," Sunny said as she led the way up the steps into the diner. "Will it work?"

"Well, it's advice from a pro. But before I agree to this we're going to establish a few ground rules."

"Such as?"

He pushed open the door. "I'll tell you while we have coffee."

"UH-OH," SUNNY SAID an hour later as Chase parked his car next to hers in front of the carriage house.

"Problem?"

"Hector left my car here. That means he wants me to track him down at the grocery store. I'll have to hurry. Thursday evenings are frantic."

The phone was ringing shrilly when they got inside. Sunny grabbed it. "Service with a Smile. Oh, hi, Mrs. Butler."

While she chatted with her customer, Chase looked around the large room that served as both office and living quarters. Everything was in order, not a paper out of place to remind him of the chaos of a few days ago. Just the empty bird cage. He ran his finger over the latch. If they'd been able to keep Gracie locked inside, she wouldn't have been hurt. He thought of the diaper pin that now adorned the door of Gracie's new cage. If only it were that easy to protect Sunny.

"I'll tell you what, Mrs. Butler, I'll ask the butcher how large a roast you'll need to feed six. Yes, I'll be sure to tell him that your daughter-in-law is a light eater. And that your grandson is a bottomless pit. No, no problem. I'll handle it personally." Replacing the receiver, she jotted down a few notes. When she glanced up, she was surprised to find Chase hadn't left. He was pacing her kitchen floor.

"I'm going to be a while," she said. "You don't have to wait."

"I'm not sure when that security firm I called will get their men here. I don't like leaving you here alone."

"It's still light out. Surely you don't—"

"I'm staying."

"Fine." Pulling an order pad out of a drawer, Sunny punched the button on the answering machine and began to check off items on the list.

For five full minutes she tried to ignore Chase. Let him waste his whole evening if he wanted to. She couldn't afford to worry about it. When the phone rang, she reached for the receiver.

"Let the machine get it," Chase said.

She frowned at him. "Why? If it's a customer, I'll just have to take it off the machine."

"You won't have to waste time chatting with a machine. It's much more efficient."

Sunny took a calming breath as she rose from her chair. "I don't consider chatting with my customers a waste of time. Some of them like to chat. Some of them need to chat. Don't you have anything more important to do than stand here and offer free critiques of the way I run my business?"

"I told you. I'm not leaving you here alone."

"Look, I already have two guardian angels watching out for me up at the house."

"And if Arnie Zimmerman decides to pay you a call? What will they do? Mow him down with a wheelchair?"

The image was too much for Sunny. She giggled. "I'd put my money on my aunts. Besides, they have a gun for backup."

"*You're kidding!*"

"Aunt Alma claims Aunt Marnie's a crack shot. I didn't ask to see the gun."

Chase strode toward her. "That settles it. It isn't enough that you're being stalked by an arsonist. Now you've got a couple of crazy old ladies with a gun just waiting for the chance to protect you! You are not going to continue to live under this roof."

"Hold it right there!" Sunny leaned forward over the desk. "I am willing to take reasonable precautions until the security people you hired nab Arnie. I even agreed to sleep at your apartment until they do. If I moved in with my aunts they'd worry too much. But I won't have you saying such things about them! I'll have you know they are perfectly sane old women. At least I think they are. They would never use the gun, even if they had it. I hope. But more importantly, the roof I choose to live under is my business, not yours." She threw her hands up in the air. "Just what do you expect me to do, anyway? Take up permanent residence on your couch?"

"We could get married."

"Married?" Sunny knew that her mouth had formed the word, but she didn't hear any sound come out. Her ears were ringing. With wedding bells? No. Impossible.

Chase, too, was speechless. Had he actually said what he thought he'd said? He was a writer. He knew about words, how to choose them and craft them to express his exact meaning. And he had just asked Sunny Caldwell to marry him.

Sunny was the first to recover. "Don't be ridiculous!" But to her own ears, her voice sounded weak, breathless. Marriage! It was the last thing she wanted, wasn't it?

Chase watched her carefully. "Not so ridiculous. We want each other. And an affair is problematic. We have the children to consider. If you stop to think about it, marriage is a very practical solution." Even as he said the words, Chase could see them appear in his mind, much the way they would appear on his computer screen. He was vividly aware that he'd never in his life strung sentences together with less grace or style.

Sunny felt the prick of tears behind her eyes. She couldn't, wouldn't cry in front of him. Not that there was any need to cry. Except for the funny pain around her heart. Lifting her chin, she said, "I prefer not to think about it. I don't have time to think about it because I have a lot of other things on my mind."

Chase said nothing as she gathered together the orders she'd been working on and began to tap the edges on the surface of the desk. She seemed so calm. It was only when the papers slipped out of her hands that he noticed she was trembling. Helplessly he watched her gather them up again.

When she left, he followed her all the way to her car. "When will you be home?"

She turned on him then, her eyes bright, her mouth set in a stubborn line as she swept her arm toward the carriage house. "This is my home. I'll be at your apartment as soon as I finish making the last delivery. And you don't have to worry. Hector will escort me there."

Chase watched her back out of the driveway, taking some satisfaction when she hit the hedge twice. But there was no escaping the fact he'd bungled it. Big time. The only question was what in hell was he going to do about it?

7

"MR. MONROE!"

Chase saw Marnie waving at him from the back door of the house.

"Do you want some tea? Alma just made a fresh pot."

He wanted to pace. He wanted to smash his fist through something. And then pace some more. With a sigh, he ran his hand through his hair. Perhaps tea would help. He walked up the steps and followed Marnie as she wheeled herself into the den. Alma gestured him toward a love seat, then leaned forward in her rocking chair to pour him a cup. "Sugar?" she asked.

He shook his head as he took the tea and sat down.

"It's so nice of you to join us. Sunny seldom has time at the end of the week," Marnie said.

Chase sipped his tea absently.

"Is it all right?" Marnie asked. "We have some regular tea bags if you prefer."

"Fine." He glanced down at his cup and set it on the table.

"It's not the tea," Alma said, giving her sister a pointed look. "The man is worried about larger issues. How did your visit with our brother go?"

Chase glanced up to find himself pinned by two very curious pairs of eyes.

Marnie gave him an encouraging smile. "We're not as naive as we look. Nothing you tell us about Leo will surprise us."

"Good heavens, no," Alma said with a laugh. "We're his sisters. We know him very well. Even as a kid, he had a taste for the finer things in life. Always wanted something our parents couldn't afford. And he usually found a way to get it."

"But there's another side to him," Marnie said. "He's always been generous with his money, especially where his family is concerned." She waved a hand. "He gave Sunny's parents the down payment on this house when they were married, and he took back the mortgage when the cancer got so bad that Sunny's dad couldn't work anymore. And most people believe he's done a good job representing this community in Albany. That's the Leo that Sunny knows. The indictment was quite a shock to her."

"But you ladies weren't surprised?" Chase asked.

Alma shook her head. "We knew him when he was collecting a percentage of the profits from every lemonade stand in our neighborhood. He wore a sign and flagged down cars. Convinced the neighbor kids he was increasing their business."

Marnie smiled. "He probably was. He's always had such a way with people." She handed Chase a delicately flowered plate with a minute sandwich on it. "What is Leo's connection to the burglar who ransacked the carriage house?"

Chase stared at the two ladies. Alma sat across from him and Marnie had positioned her wheelchair at the end of the love seat. Short of vaulting over it, he couldn't see how he could escape from the room. Resigned, he told them everything he had learned from Leo at the prison.

"Is Sunny in any imminent danger?" Marnie asked.

"Danger?"

"From this Arnie Zimmerman?"

With a start, Chase realized he'd shoved the very real danger Sunny was in to the back of his mind. Ever since he'd . . . What was the matter with him? That was why he'd blurted out that proposal, wasn't it? Because he'd wanted to protect her?

"You've taken care of everything, then?" Marnie prompted.

"I've hired a security firm to guard the carriage house twenty-four hours a day. They start sometime this evening, and they'll keep an eye on this place, too." With a sigh, he placed the sandwich plate on the table. "But I don't want her living there. She won't move in with you because she doesn't want to worry you. Besides, she might be tempted to run over there at odd times, or worse still, confront this man by herself. But I know she's not comfortable staying with me and the kids." He glanced around and saw that the ladies were very interested by his statement. "Not that we're... I mean... She's sleeping on the couch."

Marnie smiled and nodded. "We understand."

"No, really." He lifted his hands and dropped them. The more he protested, the less credible it would sound. "I—I asked her to marry me."

Marnie exchanged glances with Alma. "So that's why she almost destroyed the hedge."

"Sounds like you botched it," Alma said. "A woman needs to be courted, you know." She sipped her tea and leaned back in her rocker. "I had a beau once who used to take me out dancing every Saturday night. And each time he picked me up, he brought me yellow roses. I very nearly married him. Not that I have any regrets, you understand." She refilled her cup. "I liked men a lot in those days, but I never wanted to tie myself down to one. But those roses..." Alma sighed. "They were lovely." Meeting Chase's eyes, she said, "Take my advice. Romance is the answer. Ask her out on a date."

He never had, Chase realized. All he'd ever done was ask her to help with the children.

"If you want my opinion," Marnie said, "it's those children who hold the key to Sunny's heart. She's a modern woman, liberated, thinks she needs to be free. But if those kids were to be threatened in some way—"

"Marnie Caldwell!" Alma said.

Marnie waved her hands impatiently at her sister. "Quiet. I'm thinking out loud." She wiggled a finger at Chase. "I know. Maybe one of your security guards could stage a fake kidnapping. Just for a few days."

"I don't think—" Chase began.

"It worked on 'Santa Fe Scandals.'" Marnie looked at Alma for support. "Remember when Charlene's daughter was snatched by the man with multiple personalities?" She reached over to pat Chase on the knee. "Believe me, there's nothing like the threat of danger to cement a romantic relationship."

Alma rolled her eyes. "Kidnapping might be a little extreme." She turned to Chase. "But my sister is right about one thing. Those children are very important to Sunny. She loves them, but at the same time, she's afraid to become too involved with them."

At Chase's puzzled look, Marnie explained. "Because of her father. You see, he was an inventor."

"Brilliant," Alma added. "Put his brain to better use than Leo ever did."

"But he died before he ever got a patent on one of his inventions. Sunny has it in her head that she and her mother took up too much of his time and kept him from fulfilling his dream," Marnie said.

Alma shook her head. "Not true. Sunny and her mother were his salvation. If Leo had only had a family—"

"That's it!" Marnie clapped her hands.

Alma stared at her sister. "It's a little late for Leo—"

"I'm not talking about Leo. I'm talking about Sunny's dream." Marnie turned to Chase. "That's the way to win her heart. She wants Service with a Smile to succeed. That's why she sent you that brochure in the first place. She needs to expand her client base. If you can help her do that, then she'll realize you and the children won't be a threat to the success of her business."

"Money's no problem," Chase said.

Marnie shook her head impatiently. "No. She won't take money from you or anyone. But you could introduce her to some of your society friends."

"Business! Bah!" Alma began loading a tray with cups. "What's the world coming to when all that matters is the bottom line? I think you should sweep her off her feet." She glared at her sister. "What's the matter with you? First kidnapping, then money. You're beginning to sound like Leo."

Marnie lifted her chin. "It doesn't have to be a kidnapping. A milder threat would do. Nothing tugs on a woman's heart more than a child in jeopardy. Look at the made-for-TV movies. Look at the bestseller lists."

"Hmph!" Hefting the tray, Alma strode from the room. "I still vote for yellow roses."

Seeing an escape route at last, Chase rose, circled the table and followed her out.

As he opened the screen door and stepped out, Chase said, "Ladies, it's been . . . illuminating."

IT WAS ALMOST ELEVEN when Sunny exited the elevator and walked down the hall to Chase's apartment. She had hoped to be even later, but Hector was tired and she had promised Chase that Hector would see her to the apartment.

Letting herself in, she noticed the light fanning out from the archway to the kitchen. She felt her heart sink and her palms go suddenly damp. Chase was up. Any hope she had of avoiding him . . .

Wiping her hands on her jeans, she straightened her shoulders and walked into the kitchen. Inside the archway, she paused. He was sitting at the counter, wearing glasses, hunched over a thick book. *Lonely.* That was the word that came to mind as she walked toward him.

"I was beginning to think you'd decided to stay at the carriage house, after all."

Climbing onto the stool across from him, Sunny met his eyes directly. "The thought did enter my mind. But when Hector and I were finishing up, I started noticing every little noise." She shifted her shoulders as she recalled the feeling. "I don't know. . . . It was so dark outside the windows. The place started giving me the creeps."

"Thank God for small favors," Chase murmured fervently.

"No." She frowned. "It's not a favor. I've lived in that carriage house for five years now. It was my first home away from . . . home. Now I'm nervous there even when Hector's around."

Chase covered her hand with his. "I'm sorry."

The quick flash of understanding in his eyes warmed her. "My father used to work on his inventions there." She smiled. "Every afternoon when I got home from school, I would sneak around to the back and watch him through the window so I wouldn't disturb him. He had such big dreams."

"Some of them must have come true."

She shook her head, and her smile faded. "They might have if he'd been one of those people with tunnel vision, completely devoted to his goal. But Dad felt an equal obligation to Mom and me. So he only worked on his inventions from the time school let out until dinner was ready. And then his time ran out. But even after they diagnosed the cancer, he kept to his schedule."

Chase thought of the priority he had always given to his work and the changes Emma and Jason were making. Would he change back even if he could? "Maybe your father was happy with the choices he made."

"I don't know. The fact he never sold one of his ideas makes his life seem unfinished somehow." She felt the comforting pressure of Chase's hand. And it was only then that she realized her fingers were linked with his.

As if he was just noticing too, Chase withdrew his hand and slipped off his glasses to pinch the bridge of his nose.

He looked exhausted. Because she wanted to touch him and smooth the tired lines away, she picked up the book that lay between them on the counter. "'*How Pentagon Spending Destroyed the American Middle Class*'?" Her eyebrows rose. "Not exactly upbeat stuff."

He smiled. "I like to keep up with what's making the nonfiction bestseller list."

"Know the competition?"

"Something like that."

Sunny shook her head as she set the book down. "Give me a good mystery where they catch the bad guy. Or a romance where . . ."

. . . *the boy gets the girl.* Sunny didn't finish the sentence out loud, but she felt the heat rise in her cheeks.

"Sunny."

"Chase."

They both spoke at once. Then Chase said. "About what I said this afternoon. I'd like to apologize."

Sunny felt a little band of pain tighten around her heart.

"I realize this is a time in your life when you don't want to be tied down to a family. Especially a ready-made one. I don't know what got into me. The only excuse I can make is that I want the best for those children. My children." He hesitated for a moment, studying her. The flush that had heightened her color only seconds ago had faded, leaving her skin pale. Surely he was saying what she wanted to hear. He'd been working on the right words all day. "Anyway, I thought perhaps we could just forget it ever happened."

"Sure," Sunny said, surprised her lips had actually formed the word. She'd already forgotten it, anyway, hadn't she? Proposals were easy to forget. She did it everyday. She took a deep breath and let it out, but it didn't seem to loosen the band around her heart.

Mistaking her sigh for one of relief, Chase was confident he'd hit upon the right strategy. With a clean slate, he had an opportunity to remedy the damage he'd done earlier. With a smile, he asked, "Are you hungry? There's some leftover pizza in the oven."

Sunny shook her head. She wasn't sure she could swallow.

"One other thing," Chase said as she slid off the stool. "There's this big fund-raiser for the symphony on Saturday. I have to put in an appearance. I thought you might like to go with me."

Sunny stared at him. "Are you asking me out on a date?"

"Oh, no. I thought you might see it as a business opportunity. We'll be at the head table with the mayor and his wife. She's bound to ask what you do for a living. You can tell her all about Service with a Smile."

Of course, why would he ask her out on a date? He wanted a nanny for his children. "What about Jason and Emma?"

"Heather offered to take them. They had such a good time there on Thursday. We can pick them up on our way home."

"Okay."

"You'll go, then?"

"Sure. I'd love to go."

She sure as hell didn't look as if she'd love to go, Chase thought as he watched her leave the room. He could only hope those two aunts of hers knew what they were talking about.

"TURN," ALMA SAID.

Sunny pivoted carefully in a full circle, then pressed a hand to her stomach, hoping to settle her nerves.

"No, no." Alma tugged Sunny's hand down to her side. "You're spoiling the line of the dress. We have to make sure the hem is even." Backing up to join Marnie, she said, "Now, turn again."

Sunny did as she was told. Not only had Alma helped her choose the dress in a lightning-fast shopping trip, but she'd also altered it. And it had still taken too much time. Even more time had slipped away while Alma tried to tame Sunny's curls into a sophisticated top-knot. Hector had finally offered to make the late-afternoon deliveries by himself.

"Well, what do you think?" Alma asked.

"It's fine," Sunny said.

"Perfect," Marnie said. "Absolutely perfect. Short-ening it an inch above the knee makes all the differ-ence."

Alma grinned. "Wait'll Chase sees you."

"I did not pay a small fortune for this dress to im-press Chase Monroe." Sunny glanced down at the thin silk that molded her breasts, then fell in a shimmer to the tops of her knees. Never had she spent so much for so little dress. "It's a business investment," she in-sisted. It had absolutely nothing to do with the recur-ring fantasy she was having of bringing Chase to his knees.

"Of course, my dear," Marnie said. "And you'll get years of wear out of it. Black is so wonderfully basic."

"And sexy," Alma added. "It's going to knock his socks off."

She adjusted the thin straps that fit snugly over Sun-ny's shoulders. Suddenly her eyes lit up. "I think I have the perfect thing. A black shawl." Turning, she hurried to the door. "Spanish lace. I'll be right back."

"She's so excited about this," Marnie said, "you'd almost think this date was her idea."

"It's not a date," Sunny said as she clipped on a pair of earrings, then fingered the cascade of tiny pearls that fell just short of her collarbone. "What do you think?"

Marnie pursed her lips and studied Sunny for a min-ute. "Alma hasn't lost her eye or her taste. They're the same shade as your skin. Perfect."

Sunny moved to the couch, then thought better of sitting down and began to pace. She could almost hear the tension humming along her nerve endings, the butterflies flapping their wings in her stomach. She hadn't felt this way since her high school prom.

"There's no need to worry, you know," Marnie said. "You'll pick up a lot of business tonight."

Sunny realized with a start that she wasn't thinking about business at all.

"But it's Chase you're really worried about, isn't it?"

"No . . . yes."

"You love him."

Sunny waved her hands as if she could physically push the idea aside. "He doesn't love me." She crossed to the counter, then whirled and paced back to Marnie. "He had the nerve to propose marriage! And he didn't even mean it."

"Chase has never struck me as a man who would say something he didn't mean."

Sunny threw up her hands and continued to pace. "Well, he did this time. We were right here on Thursday when he asked me to marry him. That night he apologized and asked me to forget the whole thing."

Marnie hid a smile. "Well, it's all for the best. You don't want to marry him, do you?"

"Certainly not!" Sunny tried to ignore that little band of pain around her heart. "He doesn't want me. He just doesn't want the children to wake up one day and find me gone. He loves them so much." For a second, Sunny pressed her hands to her eyes, then dropped them. "It's ironic, isn't it? I fired the nanny. Now he would like me to replace her." She managed a smile. "A fitting retribution."

When Marnie said nothing, Sunny straightened her shoulders. "Not that I have any desire to fill the position. I know what I want in life. And right now marriage and a family would only get in the way. I want to make Service with a Smile a financial success. I want caviar and champagne. And I'm not going to settle for . . ." She raised her hands and dropped them. "I'm not going to settle for pasta dinosaurs."

"Maybe you should think about having your cake and eating it, too," Marnie said. "That's what Mariah Gallagher does on 'Gallagher's Dream.' She always manages to find true love and acquires a new fortune, to boot."

Sunny rolled her eyes. "That only happens on TV. In real life, Lila McIntyre left her two-month-old son to seek fame and fortune in Hollywood."

"But you're a lot smarter than Chase's mother was. You're more like Mariah. And you could never turn your back on—"

The doorbell interrupted anything else Marnie might have said.

"It's him." Sunny glanced at her watch. "Alma would just walk right in. It's got to be Chase."

"There's only one way to find out," Marnie said.

Slowly Sunny walked toward the door.

The moment it swung open, Chase could have sworn time stopped for an instant. Certainly his heart did. The first thing he noticed was her hair, swept smoothly back from her face. Not a curl out of place. He badly wanted to remedy that.

Sunny, too, was stunned. She hadn't thought it was possible, but in a tuxedo he was even more handsome. No—elegant was the word. Then she noticed the yellow roses. Reaching for them, she lifted them to her face and inhaled. "Yellow," she said. "My favorite. They're lovely."

She was lovely, Chase thought. Above the roses, he caught her scent. Not her usual, it slammed into him, making him think of slow sex on a hot steamy night. As she turned to walk away, the thin silk of her dress shifted, and he got a very clear impression of slender thighs, a narrow waist. Then his gaze was riveted to her back, the smooth expanse of white skin, crisscrossed by the narrowest of straps. He had to focus on breathing. Part of him wanted to turn and run. Another part wanted to reach out and grab her so that she could never walk away from him again.

"Excuse me," Alma said, nudging him aside. "I found it." When she spotted the yellow roses, she gave Chase a quick wink over her shoulder. "Nice flowers." She draped the fragile black lace over Sunny's shoulders. "Hurry along, you two. You don't want to keep the limo waiting."

"Limo?" Sunny and Marnie spoke at once. And they moved together to the door to catch a glimpse.

Chase felt some of his paralysis fade when Sunny gave him an enthusiastic grin. This was the Sunny he thought he knew.

"I've never ridden in a limousine before," she said as she slipped her arm through his and hurried him out the door. He suffered a momentary relapse, though, when she climbed in and her skirt hitched up two inches.

"Why did you do it? We could have driven in your car."

"I thought you might enjoy practicing your visualization techniques."

Why *had* he done it? Chase wondered as he watched her close her eyes and run her hands across the plush upholstery. The hands that he'd been fantasizing about since the first time he'd seen her. When she discovered the champagne and poured him a glass, he drained it in one swallow. It promised to be a long evening.

SUNNY WAS GLAD she'd come. The ballroom of the hotel was filled with people. Smiling, she tried to absorb it all, the exotic scents, the soothing sound of strings that could only be heard intermittently above the laughter and the clinking of glasses. As she glanced around, her eyes were drawn by the gleam of satin and the glitter of sequins. The rich and the not so rich, the city's movers and shakers, along with others who simply loved good music, had gathered to support the symphony.

She turned her smile on Chase.

"What's so amusing?" he asked.

"We're all so dressed up. It reminds me of prom night."

Taking two glasses of wine from a passing waiter, Chase asked, "Who did you go to the prom with?"

"Peter Devine."

The name had come very quickly, he thought as he handed her a glass. When he tried to remember his own date for the senior prom, all that came to mind was the vague image of a pretty face and long blond hair. "And was he?" he asked.

"What?"

"Divine."

She grinned. "Actually, he was, in his own way. Peter was the studious type. He wore glasses and he was tongue-tied around girls. As I recall, I had to ask him for the date."

"Because you felt sorry for him?"

"No. I asked him because I think it's a lot more enjoyable to go to a prom—" she waved her free hand "—or something like this, with a friend. There's no tension, and you can just relax and have fun. Don't you agree?"

Relax? He hadn't been able to relax since he'd first seen her in that thin scrap of silk. And "fun" wasn't exactly the word he would have chosen to describe the evening so far. The lace had slipped from her shoulder, baring a smooth, creamy expanse of skin, and he found he suddenly had to concentrate on relaxing his grip on the wineglass. He shifted his gaze to her lips before he met her eyes. Behind the teasing light, he saw saw something else. A challenge?

Oh, she was definitely playing with fire, Sunny thought as she saw the threat—or was it a promise?— in Chase's eyes. It was enough to stop the breath in her throat and send a ribbon of heat winding through her. They were in the middle of a crowded ballroom. Surely he wouldn't—

"Chase, darling!"

"Melinda," Chase managed as the tall brunette hugged him. "I'd like you to meet Sunny Caldwell." He turned to Sunny. "Melinda McGill is chairperson of the fund-raising committee.

Tucking her arm through Chase's, Melinda gave Sunny a cool smile. "So far, Chase has managed to pull in the most money. I don't know what I'd do without him." She snuggled closer. "He's like a magnet."

"I can see that," Sunny said.

Turning to Chase, Melinda said, "C'mon, I'll show you to our table."

"Sunny and I are sitting at the head table with the mayor and his wife," Chase said.

"How boring," Melinda said with a pout.

In one smooth move, he slipped away from the brunette and took Sunny's arm. "Excuse us. I think I see them."

Sunny shot him a sideways glance as he propelled her through the crowd. The grim expression on his face had her chuckling. "It must be tough work. Being a magnet."

"Shut up!"

"I mean attracting all that money. Not to mention the frills— Ouch!"

"I warned you."

Sunny shook her head. "Pinching in public. You ought to be ashamed of yourself."

"Everyone knows that Chase Monroe is absolutely shameless. But I don't recall anyone ever accusing him of pinching in public before."

Startled, Sunny found herself face-to-face with a plump woman in her early fifties. Her elegant gray silk dress was an almost perfect match for the silvery hair framing her face. But it was the warm laughter in her eyes that won Sunny's instant liking.

"I'm Sally Weston," the woman said, grasping Sunny's hand firmly in hers. "And you're . . . ?"

"Sunny Caldwell."

"I've been dying to meet the woman who persuaded Chase to put in an appearance at our little celebration." She turned to Chase. "Pinching in public, eh? Well, what can you expect from a recluse? Living like that—all your manners slip away."

"I was provoked," Chase said.

Sally threw back her head and laughed. "Let's see if we can find Bill and sit down."

They were interrupted at least half a dozen times on their way to their seats. Then Bill Weston escorted Chase to the other side of the speaker's podium, and Sunny found herself seated next to Sally.

"They always do this at the head table. Separate the boys and girls. That's why I was so happy when Chase called to say he would be bringing you." Waving over a passing waiter, Sally paused until their wineglasses were filled. Then she said, "My friends—well, my enemies too—are always telling me I'm a terrible snoop. And I am. But I'm dying to know how you met Chase. I've been trying to match him up with a nice girl ever since he moved into town."

Sunny felt her cheeks heat. "Oh, we're not a match."

"Oh?"

"We're business acquaintances. We met when his niece and nephew came to live with him."

"Chase has children living with him?"

"It's a long story," Sunny said.

Sally patted her hand. "Thank heavens. This is going to be a long evening. The food will be overcooked, the speeches overwritten. Go ahead. Tell me everything."

And Sunny did. Perhaps it was because Sally was such a good listener, or perhaps it was because she could sense that Sally had a genuine affection for Chase.

One thing led to another as the evening progressed, and sometime during dessert, Sunny found herself talking about Service with a Smile.

Sally looked at her thoughtfully over the rim of her glass. "You know, I could use a grocery-shopping service. I hate doing it myself. And our cook has such a temper. She refuses to do it, claims she's an artist.

Which I suppose she is." Lips pursed, Sally thought quickly. "Do you play bridge?"

"Not since college."

Sally's eyebrows rose. "Then it's time you brushed up your skills." She withdrew a card from her purse. "Wednesdays at noon, I play with friends. Some of them are Bill's, some mine. And several of them might be very interested in your business. Then after they leave, you can meet my cook. I'm sure we can come to an arrangement."

SUNNY WAITED only until the door of the limo closed before she turned to Chase. "How can I thank you? Mrs. Weston, Sally, invited me to play bridge with her friends." Grabbing his hand, she pulled it up to her cheek. "Isn't it wonderful?"

Wonderful was one way to describe it, Chase thought as he felt his heart skip and his pulse begin to race. Her face was flushed, her eyes dark with excitement. Lights from the street dimmed, then brightened on her skin. She looked beautiful, exotic and more desirable than he'd ever seen her.

Her skin felt so smooth beneath his fingers. Cool at first, but beginning to heat. He'd told himself he wouldn't touch her tonight. But he couldn't seem to pull his hand away, couldn't seem to stop it as it slid into her hair, loosening the pins. He gave her time to pull away, but she didn't. And she didn't utter a protest when his lips moved over hers.

She'd started this, Sunny thought as the heat shot through her. Not intentionally. But just this once, she was prepared to accept the consequences. Perhaps it was the dress that was making her feel so reckless. Or perhaps Marnie was right, and she did have something in common with Mariah Gallagher. Or maybe she'd been planning this ever since she'd seen Melinda put her hands on Chase.

Later she'd analyze it, but for now his taste was enough, warm, dark, addicting. Her arms circled his neck and drew him closer. Desire arrowed through her, its intensity only heightened by the other sensations he was bringing her. The press of his fingers at the back of her neck, the stroke of his hand up her thigh, pushing away the thin silk to cup her hip and shift her so that she was lying beneath him. Then his lips left hers. But her protest became a sigh as his mouth began to explore the skin just above where the dress skimmed her breasts.

Desire. He could taste it on her skin. And desperation, too. Almost as great as his own. She was so soft beneath him. More than anything he wanted to lose himself in her.

It took more willpower than he thought he possessed to draw away. "Sunny?" Framing her face with his hands, he looked into her eyes and found the answer he wanted.

"I want you," she murmured.

Chase shuddered with the intensity of the pleasure her words brought him. Should he have known how much he wanted to hear them? Or what they'd do to his control?

"This is crazy," he said, and was surprised at the husky sound of his voice.

"Yes." She smiled as she tugged his tie loose and then dropped it on the floor of the car.

"We can't," he protested, but the tantalizing scrape of her nails against his skin as she freed one button after another kept him from stopping her.

"We can," she whispered as she nibbled at his lower lip. "And we will. No one will interrupt us here. The driver can't see us." And all the while her clever fingers were busy, pulling his shirt free and opening his trousers. He felt the sharpness of her teeth and the flick of her tongue at his throat, and with a groan, he arched back to give her freer access.

And then she flattened her palms against his chest and moved them slowly down to his waist.

"Yes. That's it. Touch me." He heard his words and the moan of pleasure that followed them, but he hadn't been aware of thinking them first. It was almost as if his body, totally immersed in the sensations she was bringing him, had completely taken over.

"Yes. Oh, yes," he said as her fingers slipped beneath his waistband and enclosed him in a warm sheath.

For a moment he went absolutely still, burying his face in her hair and drawing in her scent. Then summoning all his strength, he levered himself away and knelt down beside her. Hands on her waist, he shifted her, raising her dress and pulling off her panty hose.

Dizzy with pleasure, Sunny watched him position her legs and begin to press himself slowly into her. Only then did she raise her eyes to meet his. What she saw— the searing heat, the longing—was enough to start her first inner convulsion. As it overtook her in an ever-widening wave of pleasure, she tightened her arms and legs around him.

Chase waited, controlling his own need, until she collapsed against him. Then he began to thrust slowly into her. But each time he sank into her silky heat, he seemed to go deeper and deeper, losing more and more of himself. Then he felt the tension begin to build within her again, tighter and tighter until with one final thrust he brought them both to a shattering release.

When he could breathe again, think again, Chase found himself sitting on the plush carpet of the limousine floor with Sunny still wrapped around him. Her breathing was even, her eyes closed. But when he tried to move her, she murmured a protest and wouldn't let go.

Immediately he felt himself stir within her.

Sunny lifted her head from his shoulder and smiled at him.

"This is crazy," he said again, settling his hands at her waist.

"Mmm, hmm," she murmured as she began to move slowly up and down on him. "But so practical. No one can interrupt us."

"Except the driver." But even as he said it he was pulling down the thin straps of her dress and freeing her breasts.

"But you're so efficient. I'm sure you told him to just keep on driving."

He had, Chase thought. But he wondered if it would have mattered. All that seemed to matter was Sunny. The quick gasp of her breath when he moved his thumbs lightly over her nipples and the way her features tightened with desire as she quickened her movements. He'd thought he'd wanted her before, but now desire was building with even more intensity.

"Crazy," he repeated as he shifted her to the soft carpet and began to drive himself into her over and over until he once more felt her tighten around him and heard her moan his name. Then he, too, lost himself in an explosion of pleasure.

They lay together on the floor of the limo while sanity gradually returned. Sunny saw the moonlight spilling through the window. Then she became aware of the plush carpet beneath her and the warmth of Chase. His cheek was pressed against hers. His breath was warm on her shoulder as it gradually became more even.

He was the first to move. Lifting his head, he said, "We've stopped." He levered himself up to the seat and began to refasten his clothes. "I think the driver's waiting for us."

"Oh, my." On her knees, Sunny searched for her shoes, locating one behind Chase's leg and the other on the seat. She slipped them on and then, kneeling, pulled up the straps of her dress and wriggled everything else into place.

"Ready?"

She glanced up to see that Chase's hand was already on the handle of the door. And he was perfectly put together, as if the last few minutes hadn't occurred. Had it been only minutes—or hours? She lifted a hand to her hair.

"It's fine," Chase said. He held out his hand.

Before she reached for it, Sunny grabbed her panty hose and stuffed them into her purse.

Dazed. That was what he felt, Chase decided as they entered his apartment building. He held her hand tightly in his and tried to analyze what he'd been feeling moments ago in the limousine. Once he sorted it all out, he would understand, and then he would know what to do. But his mind remained blank.

He glanced at her as they crossed the foyer to the bank of elevators. She looked stunned too. He'd known there was passion in her. And he'd thought he'd known what it would be like to make love to her. But he hadn't been prepared for the intensity, hadn't expected to be so overwhelmed by it. No, overwhelmed was the wrong word. He'd been totally involved in it, and somehow he had given away a part of himself. He wanted to know why.

Magical. That was the word that drifted through Sunny's mind as the elevator doors slid shut on the twinkling lights in the foyer. Something you dreamed about, only better. That was what their lovemaking had been like. With her hand still in his, she turned to look at him as the elevator glided upward. On her first visit here, hadn't she thought of him as a prince? But she knew better than to expect a fairy-tale ending. It was enough just to be with him tonight.

It was only as Chase put his key into the lock that Sunny suddenly remembered. "The children. We forgot to pick them up." She tried to pull him back toward the elevator.

"I called Heather earlier. She said they were sound asleep and suggested she keep them for the night."

Inside the apartment, they stood for a moment simply gazing at each other.

"I didn't plan for this to happen," Chase said. "At least not tonight." Lifting her hand, he began to kiss her fingers one by one. "I don't regret it."

"No," Sunny said. There would be a time for regrets, but not tonight. She'd made her decision in the limousine.

When he leaned forward to kiss her lips, she raised her hand to pull him closer, ready for the quick explosion of desire he always seemed to ignite in her. But he caught her hand and lowered it to her side.

"Slowly this time," he said. "I want to see you." He traced his finger along her jaw and down her throat to where her pulse beat. If he went very slowly, perhaps he could discover exactly what it was about her that was so different. He slipped his fingers under the thin strap of silk to free her shoulder for his mouth. "I wanted to do this at the benefit."

"I know," Sunny said. She wanted badly to touch him. But something about his touch, about the way he was looking at her, was making her weak. She was almost sure she wouldn't be able to lift her hands. And then he was leading her slowly toward the bedroom. She noticed the moonlight pouring through the windows, bathing the bed, before he teased her lips with his, offering the promise of what she had tasted before. Passion, dark and addicting. But the flavor was new this time, and impossibly sweet.

She felt the silky brush of her dress as it slipped to the floor, and finally she found the strength to lift her arms. Her hands were as gentle as his as she helped him undress.

The desire that had driven them before was still there, but it was controlled, promising a sweeter pleasure because it could be prolonged.

How long? Sunny wondered when at last they settled together on the bed and she gave herself up to the pleasure of touching him. Skin sliding over skin. The brush of a finger, the press of a palm. So this was temptation. Fascinated, she ran her hands over him, discovering the flatness of his stomach, the length of this thigh. And slowly desire built into an ache.

In the moonlight, he thought she looked fragile, her skin like delicate china. When he pushed a curl off her cheek, he felt the warmth beneath. And then he began to explore every inch of her with only his fingers at first, and then with his mouth.

Madness, Sunny thought. That was what it had been like before. But this was torture. And ecstasy. Reality narrowed to the look in his eyes when she shuddered under his touch, to the quick hitch of his breath when she ran a string of soft kisses down his chest to his hip.

He'd wanted to keep control this time, but now he felt it melting away just as surely as it had before.

"Sunny," he whispered as he threaded his fingers through her hair.

"Chase," she breathed as she wrapped her arms and legs around him. "More."

He slipped into her. and suddenly there was more. Eyes open, they watched each other as the pleasure built slowly but just as powerfully as before. Each time he moved inside her, they became more a part of each other, less a part of themselves. When at last his gasp followed hers, they were one.

8

AUNT MARNIE waved to them from the front porch when Sunny and Chase pulled into the driveway on Sunday morning. The call inviting them to breakfast had come at eight o'clock, just as they were leaving to pick up Jason and Emma at The Growing Place.

Jason had phoned at seven because he missed his uncle. It was the first night he and Emma had spent away from Chase since the funeral. At Sunny's urging, Chase had agreed to drive over and pick them up.

Pushing open the door, Sunny levered herself out of the car. The night had been endless, wonderful and sleepless. She held on to the door for support when Emma and Jason raced past her to join her aunts on the porch.

Shading her eyes, she risked a glance at Chase as he circled the front of the car. It was a mistake. He had such an annoying habit of looking so much better than she felt. Far too rested for someone who hadn't had any more sleep than she had. They had to talk. Somehow they'd never gotten around to saying much during the night. A knot began to form in her stomach just thinking about it. Then the mere touch of his hand on her arm as he guided her up the steps brought back memories of what they'd shared.

Jason waved a muffin at her from the table that Alma had set outside in the shade, but it was Marnie's offering she took—a mug of steaming coffee. The caffeine might just save her life.

It was only then that she noticed the man perched on the edge of the chaise longue. She wondered how she could have missed him. With his sharp, pointed features and round belly, he reminded her of a large, pudgy bird. With very pretty feathers, she decided as she took in the powder blue blazer and perfectly pressed slacks. He wore his grayish blond hair neatly parted in the middle and swept back from his face. And his eyes. Could that turquoise color be real? she wondered as she met his gaze over the wire rims of his glasses.

"This is Martin Shulman, Sunny," Marnie said. "A new customer. Alma found him wandering around out back."

Rising, the man placed his mug on the table and took Sunny's offered hand in both of his. "Delighted, Ms. Caldwell. Please call me Marty."

"What were you doing wandering around out back?" Chase asked with a frown.

Releasing Sunny's hands, Marty withdrew a card from his pocket. "I was looking for Service with a Smile. I drove up and down the street several times before I spotted the building at the end of the driveway." He gave Chase a worried look. "That is the place, isn't it?"

Chase glanced down at the card—one of Sunny's—and then back at Martin Shulman. "And you came on a Sunday?"

Martin raised his hands and lowered them. "I'm a desperate man. My mother fell a few days ago and broke her hip. I've been at her side ever since. A neighbor dropped by for a few hours today." He gave Sunny a pleading look. "I don't mean to intrude."

"Of course not." Sunny patted his arm. "Most Sunday mornings I do work for a little while. We'll head over to my office right now."

Chase took two steps before Sunny turned back to him. "I won't require your help, Mr. Monroe."

He scowled after them until they disappeared around the side of the house.

"She'll be all right," Marnie assured him.

"Yeah," Alma said. "He wouldn't dare attack her. He might put a wrinkle or two in those fancy duds he's wearing. Besides, you can rest assured those security men you hired will keep a sharp lookout. I took 'em some of my coffee about an hour ago."

"You what?" Chase asked.

"Gave them some coffee." Alma refilled Chase's cup.

"Oh, no." Chase sank onto the chaise longue that Marty Shulman had just vacated.

"Is there a problem?" Marnie asked.

Chase sighed. "They're supposed to be working undercover. If someone's watching this place, waiting for the chance to break into the carriage house, he probably knows now that someone else is watching it, too."

"So?" Alma demanded with a frown. "What's wrong with that? You certainly don't want someone sneaking in there to burglarize the place again."

Chase drained the coffee from his mug, then cleared his throat. "Well, actually, that was the plan. Sunny is determined to catch the guy in the act and then talk to him."

Alma snorted. "So that Leo won't get in any more trouble."

"Something like that."

"Well, you better tell those two men to bring their own food and coffee from now on," Alma said as she opened the door to the house. "I'm fixing scrambled eggs. Don't you dare talk about anything that happened last night until I'm back. I want to hear every detail."

Chase handed his mug to Marnie as soon as Alma was out of sight. "I'm going to have a talk with the two men on duty."

"WHAT A MARVELOUS PLACE," Marty said once they were inside the carriage house. He rubbed his hands together. "Simply marvelous."

"Thank you," Sunny said as she sat down at her desk and began pulling some papers from a drawer. "I'm going to show you some forms that might be helpful. Does your mother live alone?"

"Oh, my, my, my."

Sunny glanced up to find that Marty had wandered down the length of the room and was gazing out the window near Hector's computer. The man had moved as quietly as those dratted mice. And just as quickly, too. The extra weight he carried didn't seem to slow him down. "Is something the matter?"

"Oh, I'm sorry." He waved a hand as he turned back to her. "It's just the view. Breathtaking. All those trees." He clasped his hands together. "You must feel like you're living in the country."

"Almost." Sunny smiled. "The woods on that side extend into Sunnydale Park." As he drew near her desk, she held out the forms, but he walked past her to the window over the couch.

"And on this side, you can see the house of a neighbor and feel secure. Marvelous." He turned back to her. "Still, it must make you a little nervous living here alone."

"I'm not living here," she said, and then was appalled to feel the heat begin to rise in her cheeks. "Not right at the present."

"Oh?"

"I had a burglary here a week ago."

"No! How perfectly awful. You weren't hurt?"

"No."

"And the bird?"

"At Mr. Monroe's apartment." Sunny frowned. "How did you know about her?"

"The cage." He walked to it and shut the open door with one finger. Then he shivered slightly. "I can certainly understand why you moved out. After a burglary, I would be very nervous, too." He glanced up at the loft. "And a building this old must have ghosts."

Sunny shook her head. "Only mice. Would you like to look at these forms now?"

"Of course." He hurried to take the chair in front of her desk. "I do tend to get carried away when I see a place like this." He aimed a smile at her. "I'm an interior decorator, and I would just love to get my hands on it." Lifting the forms, he frowned at the desk. "This would be the first thing to go."

Sunny spread her hands protectively over the surface. "I need a place for my customers to fill out their orders." She glanced pointedly at the papers in his hand.

"Ah, yes." He stood. "Why don't I take these with me? Show them to my mother. I don't want to take up too much of your time on a Sunday."

"Really, it's no—"

The door swung open, and Chase strode in. "Are you finished?"

"Yes," Marty Shulman said, giving Chase a wide berth on his way out. "I'll call you tomorrow, Ms. Caldwell."

"But Mr. Shulman— Marty—" Before she could take two steps, Chase blocked her path.

"Let him go," he said as Marty disappeared out the door.

"You don't understand. He was more interested in this place than he was in groceries. Maybe—"

He placed his hands on her shoulders. "Relax. I asked one of the security men to follow him."

"But we had him right here. We could have talked to him."

"And you think he would have admitted he was Arnie Zimmerman?"

"Maybe not." She drew in a breath and let it out slowly. "Maybe we're just overreacting. He doesn't look like the man who chased you at the zoo."

"He could be an accomplice." Chase glanced around the room. "What did he do besides look the place over?"

Sunny's gaze moved to the bird cage. "He asked me about Gracie." Suddenly she turned to stare at Chase. "And I told him I wasn't living here anymore."

"Good."

"Good!" Sunny threw her hands up in the air. "What's good about it? If he knows that no one is living here, he's probably making plans right now to torch the place!"

"Then we'll catch him."

"And what if we don't?"

"We discussed all this that day at the diner. Hector has made backups of your records. The insurance money would replace your equipment."

"And who's making a backup of this place?"

Chase didn't answer. He couldn't.

Sunny walked to the window that faced out on the woods. She ran her hand along the sill. "This is the window I used to look through to see my father working when I was a little girl. Remember I told you? Sometimes I'd even climb through it and sit quietly and do my homework. Dad would be so wrapped up in his experiments that he wouldn't notice me. When I was finished, I would just sit there and dream."

"I used to use the attic in my father's house," Chase said. "No one ever thought to look for me there." He moved toward her. "Sunny..."

Whatever he had intended to say faded from his mind when she reached out and took his hand. Returning her grip firmly, he pulled her toward the door and flipped the lock.

"What—"

"I want you," he said, leaning against the door and bringing her close. "I've been aching for you since this morning when Jase called and we had to leave." He ran one hand from her shoulder to the back of her thigh, molding the softness of her body to the planes and angles of his own until the fit was perfect. "I can't seem to get enough of you." With his other hand, he circled her throat and used his thumb to urge her chin up.

Sunny heard the hunger in the roughness of his voice, tasted the hot, dark flavor of it as his lips crushed hers and his tongue probed the deep recesses of her mouth. She ran her hands over his shoulders and felt his hard muscles grow more tense as her own began to melt.

She managed to whisper, "The children . . ."

"Watching television with your aunts."

Summoning up all her strength, Sunny moved backward, taking him with her. "Have you ever made love on a futon?" she asked.

"A what?"

"C'mon. I'll show you." Sunny started up the ladder, then felt his hands grip her waist and turn her around.

"Hold on," he ordered as he slipped his fingers beneath the elastic at her waist and dragged her panties and sweats off. "Wrap your legs around me. Yes, like that."

With her hands gripping the rung behind and above her head, Sunny watched as he tugged open the snap of his jeans and jerked down the zipper. Then she stopped breathing as he placed his hands on her hips and pushed into her.

"Take all of me," he said as he thrust more deeply. "Yes, like that."

His fingers burned into the flesh of her hips as he withdrew slowly and then entered her again.

"Chase," she said as pleasure arrowed through her.

Once again, he drew back and then resheathed himself in her burning moistness. "Look at me, Sunny. Tell me you want me."

Sunny opened her eyes. "I want you."

He began to move in a fast, furious rhythm. Without another thought, Sunny gave herself up to the shattering sensations that only he could bring her. As she felt the tension begin to spiral through her, she dropped her arms around him and pulled him even closer, crying out his name as the final wave of pleasure broke through her.

When she opened her eyes, she was cradled in his lap and he was seated on the floor leaning against the ladder to the loft. For a moment she said nothing, trying to hold on to the moment. Then she felt his hand move softly through her hair. "Your hair," he murmured. "The color is fascinating. Each strand is different."

"My father liked it, too." She raised her head. "When I was born, he said it reminded him of the setting sun. That's how I got my name."

"It suits you." He smiled slowly. "You said something about a futon?"

She laughed. "How long was that television show?"

"Not long enough, I'm afraid. And probably not very interesting. I had to bribe them to watch it."

Sunny shook her head. "Corrupting America's youth. What did it take?"

I promised to take them to the park to fly kites."

"Big spender."

"I told them I would talk you into coming with me. That's what sold them."

Sunny's expression sobered. "We're going to have to make time to talk. I mean, what about tonight? Maybe I shouldn't stay at your place. We have to think about the children. We can't . . ." She waved a hand.

"I agree. You'll sleep on the couch. I'll stay in my room." Not that it would be easy. But she was right.

"We'll talk tonight," he promised. Then he leaned forward to place a quick kiss on her lips. "Have you ever flown a kite before?"

"I'm a pro."

"WE'D BETTER HURRY with these hamburgers." Sunny grabbed the ground beef out of the refrigerator and dumped it into a bowl. Chase was on the phone checking with the security people. "The charcoal will be ready any minute." She placed the bowl on the counter in front of Emma. "Jason put so much lighter fluid on those coals! Next time, you and I will do it."

Sunny took a handful of meat and looked at the little girl. "Want to help?"

Emma nodded.

"There's a real art to making the perfect hamburger. My father taught me. First, you have to get just enough to fit in the palm of your hand. Next, roll it around so that the edges will be neat. Then press it flat." She demonstrated against the wooden surface of the counter. Lifting her hand, she met Emma's eyes. "What d'you think?"

The little girl glanced down at the ground beef.

"Not good enough," Sunny said, pointing to the lumps. "It needs to be patted. Very gently. We don't want to pound all the juice out. Now, you try it."

She watched as Emma took some of the ground beef and began to roll it between her palms. The day had been fun. She couldn't remember the last time she'd flown a kite. And when she'd tripped and rolled down the hill, the children had laughed. Both of them. Was it then that the little bubble of panic had settled in her stomach? Or later, when an elderly couple had mistaken them for a family? Chase had promised they would talk tonight. Was she more worried about what he would say or what he wouldn't?

"Is this okay?" Emma asked.

Sunny glanced down at the hamburger patty. "Perfect." Then her eyes flew to the girl's face. But Emma was busy pulling another handful of meat free. Could she have imagined it?

Drawing in a deep breath, Sunny said, "You've done this before. This looks like the work of a professional patty patter."

Emma flashed her a grin. "Patty patter." Then she pressed another mound of ground beef against the counter. "Patty pat. Patty pat."

Sunny felt several emotions at once. She took a step forward. Then she saw Chase standing in the archway to the kitchen with Jason. He was grinning from ear to ear. She could feel, even at a distance of yards, his joy waiting to break through. And in his eyes she saw everything she was feeling, everything she wanted . . .

Jason rushed to the counter and climbed onto one of the stools. "Hey! You're talking again, Emma. That's great. Can I make one of the burgers?"

"I'll show you," Emma offered.

While Emma proceeded to instruct Jason in the art of making the perfect hamburger, Sunny turned and began to pull plates out of the cupboard. She had to keep busy, or else . . .

Chase took the plates from her and set them on the counter.

"The silver . . ."

"In a minute," he said.

She didn't know she was crying until he traced the path of a tear down her cheek with one finger. She tried to speak then, but he brushed the same finger across her lips.

"I know," he said.

"See the lump?" Emma said.

"I'll get rid of it." Jason began to pound the circle of ground beef with his fist.

Sunny and Chase turned to watch as Emma took her brother's hand and began to uncurl his fingers, one by one. "Gently," she said. "You have to keep the juice in."

Jason frowned. "How do you know so much?"

Emma lifted her chin. "Sunny and I are professional patty patters. Right, Sunny?"

Sunny grinned. "Definitely. And we'd better get some of them cooked. What do you two like on your hamburgers?"

"Mustard," Jason replied.

"Catsup," Emma said. "It still has a lump."

Jason frowned. "It does not."

"Does, too. See?"

"Does not."

"Is this what we have to look forward to?" Chase asked Sunny in an undertone.

Sunny laughed. "Isn't it wonderful?"

"Yes. Yes, it is." Leaning against the counter, Chase watched Sunny judge the merits of the flattened patty. He'd never felt so at home.

LATER, CHASE STOOD on his balcony looking out over the city. The sky was darkening quickly, and more and more drivers were turning on their headlights. Day was losing the battle with night, and he was losing Sunny.

The panic had begun to build when he was standing in the bedroom doorway listening to the children arguing over the light princess. Emma had chosen the story, but Jason was taking every opportunity to inject blood and gore.

It had hit him quite suddenly, while Sunny was negotiating a minor detail of the story with Jason, that she might no longer feel any obligation to stay. Oh, she wouldn't move back to the carriage house just yet. Certainly not until they settled the matter of Arnie Zimmerman. But then what hold would he have over her? Emma was talking, and Jason seemed to be adjusting well.

He recalled the way she'd tilted her head to laugh at something Jason had said, and how her eyes had met his for just a moment. He'd felt the pull, the tug of attraction that he'd experienced from the very beginning. But it was more than that. Desire, he could understand, even control. But what he wanted from Sunny went far beyond that.

He loved her.

The realization had sent him to the balcony. To breathe. To think.

He leaned against the iron railing and inhaled the familiar smells of the city. Gas and tar, and over that the smoky scent of grilled meat. The downtown streets had few cars, but from beyond the nearby buildings where the expressway bisected the city, he could hear the muted sounds of traffic, the occasional blast of a horn, the rumble of a tractor trailer.

Love. Was that what he'd been feeling when he'd blurted out that pitiful proposal of marriage? Was that why he'd been driven to listening to the advice of her two eccentric aunts? And he'd done more than listen. He'd actually followed it.

Oh, he was definitely in love. But what was he going to do about it? Sunny had made it quite clear that the last thing she wanted was an instant family. What good was it going to do to give her champagne and limousines one night, and hamburgers and colas the next six?

"Chase?"

Turning, he saw her standing in the open doorway to the balcony. In the moonlight, her hair looked darker, her skin paler, like fine porcelain, smooth and cool to the touch. But he knew he had only to run the tips of his fingers over it to feel it heat. Her beauty quite simply took his breath away.

"Why did you leave?" She moved toward him, and he saw the concern in her eyes. "You've done that before. Walked out of the room when I was finishing a story. I don't mean to take your place with them."

The urge to reach out to her was so strong he wrapped his fingers around the iron railing. "You don't. You have your own place with them. A very special one. If it weren't for—"

"No." There was impatience in her voice. "Don't shortchange yourself. It's because of *you* that Emma's talking now. You love her. And you love Jason. Unconditionally. I saw it that first night. Those children know that. They can feel it. And it's their strength."

"You love them, too."

Sunny waved her hand. "Whatever I've added has been frosting on the cake. And who wouldn't love them? They're wonderful kids."

"Yes." Chase turned to look at the city again. Street-lights lined the roadways, and a few stars winked on overhead. "They had wonderful parents."

"You've never spoken of them," Sunny said as she joined him at the railing.

"David was five years my junior. His mother was my father's third wife. The marriage didn't last much longer than any of my father's did, but they both loved him. We all did. After the divorce, David and I only had the summers together. Usually we were at my father's place on Cape Cod with the servants. It was something we never stopped doing, even when we grew older."

"What was Laura like?" Sunny asked.

"Lovely. David met her his last year in college. He told me he knew even then that it was forever, that she was the person he was going to spend the rest of his life with. I didn't believe him at first."

"Why not?"

Chase turned to look at her. "I found it difficult to believe that someone who was my father's son would view marriage as a lifetime commitment." Even in the fading light Chase could see the question in Sunny's eyes. How could he explain his father and the continuous string of women in his life? "After a few glasses of wine, my father once compared his relationships with women to a roller-coaster ride with breathtaking heights and frightening lows, exhilarating while it lasted, but eventually and inevitably coming to an end."

"And did your mother agree with his definition?"

"No." His lips curved slightly. "My mother never intended to get married at all. That's probably what attracted my father to her in the beginning. Lila McIntyre never had any desire to become Mrs. Chase Monroe II. She has always been totally focused on her next career goal and how to achieve it. I think I was the only thing in her life that wasn't planned. But she managed even that."

"By leaving you with your father." Just thinking of Lila McIntyre made a knot form in her stomach. Sunny covered Chase's hand with hers. "Do you hate her?"

"No. I admire her. She knew what she wanted when she was eighteen and she went out and got it." He studied Sunny for a moment and saw the flash of fire in her eyes that told him she was ready to do battle for him. "You're a little bit like her in that way."

Sunny's eyes widened. The "Gallagher's Dream" vignette of Lila McIntyre being slowly unwrapped from her red feather boa popped into her mind. "Red isn't my color."

He reached out to tuck a loose curl behind her ear. "Red is your very best color."

Sunny felt her pulse skip and then race. Somehow her fingers had become linked with his. There was a strength about him she could see in his face and feel when their hands were joined. The children sensed it, too. How in the world was she going to walk away from it? Did she even want to? She didn't back away when he stepped closer and then turned so that she was trapped in the corner of the balcony. "Chase, we can't . . . What if the children wake up?"

"Just a kiss. I've been wanting this for hours. Kiss me."

Sunny raised herself on her toes to do just that. How could she refuse when she wanted it so much? As soon as their lips met, she felt the burning excitement he always brought her. And then his taste poured through her, hot and sharp. Exactly what she'd come to crave.

As she found the hem of his shirt and slipped her hands beneath to run them up his back, she felt his quick intake of breath, his involuntary shudder. The wave of weakness that washed over her was followed this time by a rush of power.

Chase dragged his mouth from hers only to breathe. But her scent, her taste, drew him back. He found the sweetness of honey on her lips, then a sharper, hotter flavor as his tongue moved over hers. His hunger built along with his need. His hands seemed to move with a will of their own, as if they, too, were starved for the softness of her breasts, the melting silkiness of her skin.

"Uncle Chase!"

As the sound of his name penetrated his mind, Chase managed to pull away. He shook his head to clear it, then stepped back to lean against the balcony railing for support.

"Uncle Chase, Sunny, hurry! Gracie's out of her cage!"

Sunny opened her eyes and tried to focus on the two children standing in the open doorway to the living room. "Where?" she asked, amazed that her lips could form the word. The air was chilly in contrast to the heat she'd felt only seconds before.

Chase was the first to move, pushing himself forward three steps to where Jason stood.

"In the kitchen," Jason said, leading the way through the sliding glass door.

"The hallway," Emma said.

"Close the doors," Sunny said.

But before Chase could usher the children off the balcony, the bird flew out, circled and settled for a second on his head. The instant Chase raised his hand, she was off, landing briefly on the railing, then flying upward.

"She's on the roof," Jason said, craning his neck.

"Look!" Emma pointed a finger.

"Shh," Sunny said. "We don't want to scare her away."

"Buenos días," Gracie said from her perch.

"Buenos días," Sunny replied, walking slowing toward the railing where the bird could see her more clearly. "Good girl." Lifting her hand, she crooked her finger. "C'mon. Good girl."

Gracie remained where she was.

"C'mon, Gracie. Good girl." Sunny wiggled her fingers.

The bird hunkered farther down on the decorative cornice that edged the roof of the building.

"Keep talking to her," Chase muttered as he gave the railing a yank to test its stability. Then he swung his left leg over it and placed his foot on the narrow cement ledge that bordered the balcony.

Sunny shot him a worried look and whispered, "What are you doing?"

"I'm going to rescue the damn bird. Keep talking to her."

"You can't," Sunny said. Then her eyes widened in horror as she watched him swing his other leg over.

"Que sera, sera," Gracie said, flapping her wings.

"Talk to her," Chase hissed as he wiped first one palm and then the other against his pants. He lifted one foot to the top of the iron railing. Then he fixed his eyes on

the cornice and without giving himself time to think
about the sixteen-floor drop, he shifted his weight forward and sprang upward to grip the edge of the roof.

Sunny felt her heart plummet. "Chase…" The word
was barely a whisper.

"Talk to the bird," Chase said as he found his balance.

"Good girl, Gracie." She had no idea where she was
getting the breath to speak. "C'mon." She wiggled her
fingers again.

Chase tried to tilt his head back to get a better look,
then decided against it. "Where is she?"

"To your left," Sunny said in the same tone of voice
she was using to coax the bird. "About six inches."

Very carefully Chase moved his left hand along the
edge of the cornice. Suddenly a section crumbled away
in his hands.

Startled, Gracie lifted and then settled again.

Chase heard the rattle of stones hitting the balcony
floor and tried to block the image of the other pieces
falling to the street below. What in the world was he
doing? Head down, he took a deep, steadying breath.

Sunny couldn't breathe at all. To keep herself from
reaching out to Chase, she put the palms of her hands
together and prayed. If he fell … *No,* she wouldn't let
herself think about it. But she could picture it so clearly.
On either side of her, the children pressed closer.

Tightening his grip on the thin ledge of cement and
hoping it would hold, Chase risked a glance upward.
Gracie had landed inches away. Crooking the finger of
his left hand the way he'd seen Sunny do so often, he
said, *"Buenos días."*

Holding his breath, he moved his hand ever so slowly toward the bird. Relief poured through him as his fingers closed around Gracie's fragile claws. She flapped her wings, once, twice and then stopped. *"Buenos días,"* she said.

"You saved her!" Jason said.

Sunny had to grab the boy's shoulder to keep him from jumping up and down. It gave her something to do with her hands rather than reach out for Chase. She couldn't take the chance, for any movement from her might send him pitching to the pavement below. She braced her feet as the thought spun its way through her mind. And then suddenly he dropped beside her onto the floor of the balcony.

Jason and Emma each wrapped themselves around one of his legs. Sunny slid her arms around his neck and held him tight. Only as his heart beat fast and strong against her ear did she remember to breathe.

"You saved her!" Jason said. "You're lots better than that dumb guy in the fairy tale."

As she lifted her eyes to Chase's, Sunny couldn't have agreed more.

Chase cleared his throat. "Let's put Gracie back in her cage." Before he forgot all about her and she got loose again.

"Jason let her out," Emma announced as she led the way through the sliding glass doors.

"Did not!" Jason said.

"Did, too! I saw you."

Sunny kept an arm around Chase as they followed the children into the living room. When Gracie was back in her cage, Chase said, "Sunny, you tuck Emma in. Jase and I are going to have a little talk."

All the time she was settling the little girl, Sunny was thinking of Chase. And the fall he might have taken. It was a subdued Jason who joined them.

When she pulled his covers up, he put his arms around her. "Sorry, Sunny. Uncle Chase told me we could have lost Gracie for good."

But it wasn't Gracie she was thinking about as she hugged Jason and assured him that everything was all right.

She found Chase in the living room locking the balcony door. Walking to him, she put her arms around him and held him close. She didn't shut her eyes. She was afraid she would see again the image of him falling. Finally, with her cheek pressed against his chest, with his hand in her hair, the terror she'd been keeping inside began to drain away.

There was something new, Sunny thought, in the way he was holding her. His arms hadn't moved to press her closer, and yet she was more aware of their strength than ever. Perhaps the difference was in herself. Always before she'd been afraid to rely on his strength. Afraid to let herself need it. And when she lifted her head, she could see something different in his eyes. He'd never looked at her quite that way before. As if he was asking for something.

Then he pressed his mouth to hers. Softly. The kiss was not at all like the others they'd shared. There was none of the teasing or the demand she'd come to expect. His lips were gentle, careful, and yet she trembled and felt something deep inside give way.

"Sunny." He whispered her name. Had she ever heard him say it quite that way before?

He drew back, taking her hands and holding them. "There's something I have to say to you."

"Yes?"

Chase sighed and shook his head. "I work with words all the time, but somehow with you I can never find the right ones. I—"

The doorbell rang.

"Damn!" Chase said.

"Who could it be?" Sunny glanced at her watch. "It's almost nine."

"Hector."

"Hector? Why? Did you send him to Mimi's Gourmet Shop again?"

"No. Mr. Shulman gave our security guard the slip sometime late this afternoon. I found out while you were making the hamburgers. I called Hector then."

Puzzled, Sunny followed Chase down the hallway, then stared in disbelief when he opened the door. "Hector?" At least she thought she recognized her assistant beneath the frizzy gray wig and the well-padded dress. The effect was slightly spoiled by the high-top basketball shoes he was wearing. Her gaze returned to Hector's face. "It's a little early—or late—for Halloween, isn't it?"

Hector glared over Sunny's head at Chase as he tossed him a bundle of clothes. "I don't want to talk about this. I don't know why I ever agreed to it."

Sunny's eyes narrowed as she whirled around to Chase. "What's going on?"

"Hector will explain," Chase said, turning and heading for his bedroom. "I have to get ready."

"Ready for what?" she called after him, then faced Hector again. "Ready for what?"

"A stakeout."

Hands on hips, Sunny backed him into a wall. "Explain."

Hector muttered in Spanish as he raised both hands, palms out.

"In English," Sunny said, poking a finger into his chest.

"It was Chase's idea. He thinks there's a good chance Mr. Shulman or Zimmerman will make a move tonight. And your aunt Alma blew the security firm's cover." Sunny opened her mouth, but he held up a hand to stop her. "It's a long story. Ask your aunts. So Chase talked me into this masquerade. I hid in the van and got into this outfit while Alma and Marnie drove to a restaurant for dinner. They've arranged for a friend to pick them up later and take them home with her. Then I drove over here to pick up Chase. As soon as he gets ready, we go back to the house as Alma and Marnie, and we watch. And if we're lucky, catch us a firebug."

Chase appeared at the end of the hallway, tugging down the dress he'd put on. "I can't fasten the buttons."

"Doesn't matter," Hector said, grabbing his arm and pulling him toward the door. "It's dark. And you'll be in the wheelchair."

Sunny latched on to Chase's other arm. "Wait a minute! You hatched this little plot while I was making hamburgers and you didn't think to tell me?"

"I forgot when Emma started talking. Besides, there's no part for you to play. Only two people live in that house. Your aunt Alma." He pointed at Hector. "And your aunt Marnie." He pointed at himself.

"I'm coming with you," Sunny said.

"You can't." They both spoke at once.

"You have to stay with the children," Chase said.

Sunny opened her mouth and shut it as the two men left. Then she marched over to the door and gave it a good kick.

9

"WHERE ARE THEY?" Sunny demanded as she walked into her aunts' den the next morning.

Marnie poured tea into a cup and set it in front of her niece. "When they came over to drop the van off, Mary McAllister invited them in to sample some of her famous flapjacks."

"Famous my foot!" Alma said.

"They did win a ribbon at the state fair."

"Only because she flirted with the judge."

Sunny gave a sigh of exasperation. "Wait a minute, let me get this straight. They're eating flapjacks, and I had to settle for Bluegaloos."

"What are Bluegaloos?" Marnie asked.

"It's the kind of disgusting thing you eat if someone—whose name I won't mention—leaves you to look after his kids while he goes gallivanting off on an adventure."

"Well, if it's any consolation, they didn't look like they'd had much of an adventure when they arrived at Mary's," Marnie said.

"That's beside the point." Sunny rose and began to pace. "The real point is that I was left behind with the children. Again. Just as if I was . . . their nanny."

"Drink your tea," Alma urged her. "Maybe I'll enter the recipe for that in the state fair."

Sunny lifted the cup and drained it.

"What do you think?" Alma asked.

"I think Chase Monroe III is a jerk!"

"I mean about the tea."

Sunny frowned at her empty cup. It might have tasted like turpentine for all she knew. "It's great." Then, biting back another sigh, she sank onto the arm of the chair.

Marnie poured more tea. "It's more than last night that's bothering you."

"I love him." The words were out before Sunny had even fully formed the thought in her mind.

"That's wonderful!"

"It's terrible." Sunny made a face as she set down her cup.

Alma's forehead wrinkled in a frown. "You said the tea was great."

"It's not the tea that's terrible. It's the fact that I love Chase." Sunny pressed her hand against her stomach, against the panic that was building. Each time she said the words, it became more real.

"Why is loving Chase so terrible?" Marnie asked.

Sunny rose and began to pace. "It's not what I want. After Mom got married, I thought I could finally devote my life to Service with a Smile."

"And then your uncle Leo got busted," Alma said.

"But things had settled down. Everything was running so smoothly."

"Life never runs smoothly for very long, my dear," Marnie said.

Sunny stopped at the window to look out at the carriage house. "It just won't work. The children. I love them, too. But I don't want a family right now."

"Of course you do," Marnie assured her. "What you refuse to understand about your father is that his family was part of his dream, not a separate thing that kept him from achieving it."

"She's right, you know," Alma said. "Without you and your mother, your father might have ended up like Leo. Love and a family brings out the best in a person. Lord knows where old Leo would be without all of us."

At the sound of the car pulling up the drive, Sunny hurried toward the door. "They're here. I have a few words for them."

But it was only Hector who climbed out of the car. He was yawning and looked as though he hadn't slept for days.

"Chase?" she asked.

Hector yawned again. "I drove him back to his apartment. He was dead on his feet."

"And you're not?" Sunny looked him up and down. "You must have had a pretty bad night."

Hector managed a weak grin. "I won fifteen dollars from him playing gin."

"And tonight?"

"He'll have a chance to win it back. Unless your burglar shows up." Hector took one step away from the car before Sunny pushed him back.

"Go home and get some sleep. Monday's are slow. I'll manage."

"QUE SERA, SERA," Gracie said.

Sunny tapped a finger on the door of the bird cage. "Exactly. And what will be is that you're going to stay right here until Hector comes to supervise your flight time. And I don't want any surprises just because I forgot the diaper pin." Sunny leaned over to pull a can of cola out of the refrigerator. Transporting Gracie from the apartment to her office was a nuisance, but at least here, Sunny didn't have to worry about one of the children accidentally letting her go.

Frowning, she flipped up the metal top on the can and took a long swallow. There'd been no word from either Hector or Chase all day. Not that she'd expected any. Walking back to her desk, she set the can down. After all, they needed their sleep. Still, she could phone Chase. Her gaze moved to the phone. But each time she thought of dialing his number, she remembered the determined look he'd had in his eyes just before Hector had interrupted him last night.

With a shake of her head, she picked up the order form she'd been working on and then frowned. It was filled with doodles. She wadded it into a ball. Was she purposely avoiding a conversation with Chase? She began to pace the length of the carriage house. At Hector's computer, she paused to stare out the window at the woods. The view did not have its usual calming effect.

What was she afraid of? If Chase proposed again, she could always refuse. With a scowl, she tossed the crumpled ball of paper against the wall. Was she wrong in wanting to put her business first? She thought of what he'd said to her on the balcony the night before, that she was like his mother in a way. In what way? Could she really turn her back on Chase and those two children? Did she want to?

The ringing of the phone interrupted her train of thought. Running back to her desk, she lifted the receiver. "Service with a Smile."

"Ms. Caldwell, I was so hoping to find you in."

"Mr. Shulman?"

"Marty, please."

"I'm so glad you called. I never took down your phone number, and I wanted to apologize for Mr. Monroe's rudeness yesterday. You see—"

"No need. I'm sure he was simply concerned about your recent burglary. Oh, my, just the thought is enough to make me shiver. Perfectly understandable. His concern, that is."

"You're very kind." Sitting down at her desk, Sunny picked up a pencil and pulled one of her order blanks closer. "I was hoping I could meet with you again. If I could just have your address . . ."

"You're a mind reader, Ms. Caldwell. That's exactly why I called. Mother's been having one of her bad days. And she was wondering—of course I was wondering, too—if you would mind stopping by our place this evening. I know nothing about sizes and ounces—that sort of thing. Perhaps if you drove out here, you could take a look at Mother's pantry. See what she's used to?"

Sunny glanced at her watch. "What time?"

"We were thinking of between seven and eight," Marty said.

"Fine."

"We live a ways out in the country. It would be best if I met you at the corner of Flowers Road and Route 20. Shall we say at seven-thirty?"

AT EIGHT O'CLOCK, Sunny was parked in her van at the intersection Marty had named. But no one had joined her. She tapped her fingers on the steering wheel and tried to convince herself she wasn't being stood up. She hadn't told Hector or Chase where she was going. After being excluded from their stakeout, the idea of dealing with Marty Shulman on her own had been too tempting. But she was beginning to have second thoughts.

With a sigh, she picked up the receiver on her car phone and punched in the Service with a Smile number. Maybe by this time Marty had called to leave a message on the machine. But it wasn't Marty's voice on the machine; it was Chase's.

"Sunny, come to the apartment at once. It's an emergency."

The children. She felt panic shoot through her and and settle in her stomach as she made a quick U-turn with the van. She'd gone ten miles before she remembered she could call Chase's apartment on her phone.

"Monroe residence."

"Jason, is that you? Are you all right?"

"Hi, Sunny. You're missing all the fun."

"What fun? Is Emma all right?"

"Miss Caldwell is so funny. You should see her."

"Aunt Alma?" Casey asked. "What's wrong with her?"

"Uncle Chase is fixing her coffee. And he made her sit down. She was bumping into the walls."

Sunny took the phone away from her ear for a moment as it produced a wave of static. She heard Jason's giggle again before the connection went. When she redialed, the line was busy. Muttering under her breath, she pressed the accelerator and headed for the nearest highway back to the city.

The first sound that greeted her when she entered Chase's apartment was Jason's giggle. And she smelled food. Garlic and something heavenly. Her stomach growled in anticipation as she let the scent lead her to the kitchen.

In the archway, she stopped and stared. Chase and the children were seated at the counter devouring a pizza still hot enough for the cheese to form long strings as Chase lifted a slice from the box.

"Hungry?" he asked. The look he sent her had her swallowing all the questions that had been on the tip of her tongue.

"Starved," she said, climbing onto a stool and accepting the pizza. And she was, she realized as she took a generous bite and let the flavors explode in her mouth.

"Aunt Alma's taking a nap," Chase explained when she met his eyes again.

Jason and Emma burst into laughter.

"You shoulda seen her," Jason said. "She can juggle oranges. Sort of."

Sunny raised her brows, but Chase merely shook his head.

Picking up her pizza, Sunny decided that if she couldn't satisfy her curiosity, she might as well satisfy her appetite. "This is delicious."

"Emma got to order it," Jason explained, wrinkling his nose. "That's why it's only got cheese on it."

"My favorite," Emma said.

"Mine, too," Sunny assured her.

"Plain pizza is wimpy," Jason said, helping himself to another piece.

"Is not," Emma said.

"Is, too," Jason insisted.

"No arguing," Chase reminded them. "Remember our deal."

"Deal?" Sunny asked.

"Next time Jason gets to order the toppings."

"I'm going to get pepperoni and mushrooms," Jason said, leveling a taunting look at his sister.

Emma shrugged. "I'll just pick them off."

Jason frowned. "You could have done that this time."

Over the heads of the bickering children, Sunny met Chase's eyes and smiled. Then she stuffed another bite of pizza into her mouth. And a traitorous thought slipped into her mind—she wouldn't have traded it for all the pâté and champagne in the world.

AS SOON AS they were through eating, Chase managed to bribe the children into their beds by moving the television and the VCR into their room. The scuffle over which movie to watch had been settled by the toss of a coin. But it was only when they were totally absorbed that Chase led Sunny down the hall into the living room.

Alma was sound asleep on the couch. As Sunny hurried toward the older woman, she caught the pungent odor of alcohol. Praying she was mistaken, she felt Alma's forehead. "Is she ill? Should we call a doctor?"

"She's sleeping off half a bottle of sherry."

Sunny's eyes widened in horror even as she saw the evidence sitting in plain view on a table near her aunt's head. "The children?"

"They were fine," Chase hastened to assure her. "When I came home, she was entertaining them by juggling oranges. They thought she was putting on some sort of clown act."

On the couch, Alma snored softly and rolled over.

"C'mon." Chase took Sunny's arm and drew her out to the kitchen.

"I don't know what to say," Sunny said. Feeling the need to sit down, she headed toward one of the stools, then decided against it and began to pace. "I've never seen her like that. I didn't know she drank." She turned to face him. "Of course I didn't know that she didn't, either. Oh, my God." She climbed onto the stool, propped her elbows on the counter and rested her head in her hands. "She's my aunt. I mean it's not the first question that pops into your mind." Sunny dropped her hands and stared across the room. "She used to throw big parties for Uncle Leo. Do you think she got drunk at them?"

"No. I'm sure she didn't."

"How can you be sure? This is all my fault."

"And how do you figure that?"

"You hired her on my recommendation."

"So?" He walked around the counter to pull a bottle of wine out of the refrigerator.

Sunny got off the stool to follow him, pulling his arm so that he had to face her. "I fired the nanny." She felt the tears begin to build behind her eyes. "I'll bet *she* had impeccable references. She probably never had a drink in her life."

Taking Sunny by the shoulders, Chase led her back to the stool. "Sit. And get this straight once and for all. I'm the one who fired Mrs. Winthrop—I phoned and confirmed it. Now, I'm going to pour us some wine." He filled two glasses and handed one to Sunny. "Drink."

When she'd taken a sip, he said, "Again." Then he took a long swallow from his own glass before he continued, "This is not your fault."

"Yes, it is," she insisted, staring into her wineglass. "If I hadn't—"

"Your aunt Alma's little performance tonight is all part of a misguided plot to get you to reconsider my proposal."

It took a moment for the words to register, but when they did, Sunny's head snapped up, and she stared at Chase. "What are you talking about?"

Chase sighed and took another sip of his wine. How much should he tell her? he wondered. Setting his glass on the counter, he sat on the stool across from her. "I'm talking about the advice I received from your two aunts."

Sunny's eyes narrowed. "Explain."

"The day I asked you to marry me, Marnie invited me in for tea." He began to turn the stem of the glass between his fingers while he considered just how to edit what had occurred that day.

"So?" Sunny pressed. Suddenly her eyes widened. "Aunt Alma didn't spike the tea?"

Chase shook his head and decided to tell her everything. "No." He took her hands in his. "They gave me advice on how to persuade you to marry me. Alma's a romantic. She suggested yellow roses and an evening out."

"Aunt Alma?"

Chase nodded. "Marnie had two suggestions. She thinks that one way to your heart is through your business. She advised me to introduce you to prospective clients. Show you what a valuable asset I could be in making Service with a Smile a success."

Sunny stared at him. "And her other suggestion?"

"Oh, it was much more dramatic. I was to stage a kidnapping like the one that occurred on 'Santa Fe Scandals.' Alma thought that might be just a little extreme. I have a pretty good hunch that a tipsy babysitter might be a compromise."

Sunny opened her mouth and shut it as her mind raced. It all made a surrealistic kind of sense. She could easily picture her two aunts sipping tea and proposing their mad-hatter schemes to Chase. She blinked and looked at him again. And he'd actually done what they'd suggested. "Why did you follow their advice?"

"God only knows." Chase lifted his glass and drained it. "Maybe they did spike the tea."

"Whose idea was the limo?"

"Mine."

Sunny felt a bubble of laughter begin to build. "Nice touch."

He studied her, his eyes narrowed. "You think this is funny?"

She pressed her lips together and bit down hard on the inside of her cheek.

Chase frowned. "You *do* think this is funny."

Pressing a hand against her stomach, Sunny tried to keep the laughter from escaping, but it was no use. "I'm sorry," she said when she finally managed to catch a breath. "I'm sorry. Really I am." She reached for her wine. "It's just that when I think of you sitting there drinking tea, I . . ."

Chase rescued the glass, and Sunny collapsed on another wave of giggles. He couldn't decide whether to join her or strangle her. Even laughing as she was now, with that teasing light in her eyes, she could send ripples of need shooting through him.

"Tell me, what did you think of the tea?"

"The tea?" Chase asked, wondering what that had to do with anything.

She pointed an accusing finger at him. "You didn't really drink it, did you? 'Fess up."

He grabbed her hand and pulled her off the stool. "It tasted like dried weeds mixed with paint thinner. And now that you've brought it all back to me you're going to pay." Her lips were still curved in a smile when he pressed his own against them. But they softened and heated instantly.

Soft, warm, ripe, her mouth met his demands and then pulled and pulled, until everything he wanted was centered there.

He felt the edge of the counter behind his back as he drew her closer. Threading his fingers through her hair, he adjusted the angle of the kiss so that he could taste more, demand more. The fire flashed through him without warning. All he could smell was the lemony scent of her hair. All he could taste was the honey sweetness of her mouth. Suddenly desperate, he ran his hands from her hair to her shoulders and down her back to press her even closer.

Neither of them heard the ringing of the phone. It was Jason's voice that finally penetrated and had them drawing slowly apart.

"Uncle Chase. Uncle Chase, it's for you."

Sunny leaned against one of the stools for support as she watched Chase walk through the archway to pick up the phone in the hall. How could he do that? she wondered. Her own knees felt like water.

"Do you like kissing Uncle Chase like that?" Jason asked.

Brushing the curls off her forehead, Sunny looked down at the little boy. "Uh, yes." Although *like* seemed much too mild a word.

Jason wrinkled his nose. "It's awfully mushy. But Mom and Dad used to like to kiss that way a lot. Are you going to marry Uncle Chase?"

Sunny blinked. "I don't know." And she realized it was the truth. When had she become so unsure? After all the time she'd spent trying to convince herself how unwise it would be.

"It'd be nice if you did," Jason said.

Sunny felt the love bubble up. Kneeling down, she gathered the boy into her arms for a hug. How could she possibly have thought she could walk away from these children? From Chase?

After a moment, Jason wiggled away. As Sunny rose, she saw Chase standing in the archway. Alone again, she thought.

"Do you like mushy stuff like kissing, Uncle Chase?"

Chase ruffled the boy's hair. "Yeah."

Jason shook his head. "I suppose it's all right if you marry her." Then he ran down the hallway.

The words hung in the air between them for a few moments. Sunny felt the adrenaline sprint through her system. She wanted to run away. Or at least pace. Resisting the urge, she walked slowly toward Chase. "Since you proposed the last time, I suppose it's my turn. Will you marry me?"

Chase stared at her. Would he ever figure her out? From the beginning, she had confused him, intrigued him and driven him almost crazy with wanting. His gaze moved over her, noting the determined look in her eyes, the lift of her chin. He took her hands. "We're going to have to talk about this, but not—"

At the "but," she moved away. "You don't want to marry me."

"No." He shook his head. "No, that's not what I mean."

Sunny gave in to the urge to pace. "I know when you asked before that I said I preferred not to think about it—marriage, that is." She waved a hand as she circled around the counter and stools. When she turned to face him again, her heart was pounding so hard she pressed her hand against it to try to still it. "But I've thought about it a lot. I didn't think it was what I wanted or what you needed. I didn't think I could solve your problems." With another wave of her hand she continued to pace. "I mean, ideally you need someone who would stay home and devote a hundred percent of her time to the children."

He took a step toward her, but she raised both hands, palms out. "No, let me finish. It's just that maybe we could be what we each needed. I've been thinking about it. And it might work out."

Chase stared at her as she rambled on about what they each needed from the other. Did she even have a clue about what he needed and why he needed? Her and no one else. Suddenly he wanted to shake her. He wanted to make love to her until she ached with the same kind of need he was feeling right now.

"Maybe Aunt Marnie and Aunt Alma are right. They've said I need a family. That I'm like my father in that way. After all, I'm practically living here now. And it's not so bad, is it?"

Chase felt the anger whip through him and explode into a word. "No."

Sunny stopped pacing, her smile wavering a little at the force of the word. "I know it's not a perfect solution, but—"

"No, I won't marry you."

When his words registered, they had her taking a step back, then another. When she bumped into the counter, she reached for her wineglass, closing her fingers around the stem.

Struggling for control, Chase walked to the window. "I'll be damned if I'll marry you just to get a mother for Jase and Emma. They're very happy at The Growing Place, and your aunt Alma's been fine until tonight. I'll have a talk with her when she sobers up."

Sunny felt each word like a blow. She couldn't have replied if her life had depended on it. She wasn't even aware when the glass she had been holding slipped through her fingers to the floor.

Frowning, Chase started toward her, but the doorbell rang. "Damn!" he said. "It's Hector. He just phoned to say he was on his way." He swore as the second peal of the bell sent him hurrying out of the room.

The two men were on their way out when Sunny made it to the hallway. "You're going to the stakeout, right? Wait. I'm coming with you."

"No," Chase said. "You can't leave the children."

"I most certainly can. Aunt Alma is . . ." Even as her sentence trailed off, the sound of her aunt's snoring drifted into the hall. "Hector . . ."

"Hey." Hector raised both hands, palms out. "I don't want to get in the middle of this. Bad enough I've got to wear a dress."

"You wouldn't if you'd stay here and let me take your place," Sunny said.

"Not a chance," Chase said. "You aren't strong enough to get me in and out of the van in the wheelchair." Then he grasped her shoulders and gave her a quick kiss on the mouth. At least he'd meant it to be quick. But her taste, her scent, poured into him and instantly pulled him under. His head was spinning when he broke away.

Hector cleared his throat. "It's getting dark."

Chase dropped his hands to his sides. "We'll talk when I get back." Then he turned and strode toward the elevator. He could cheerfully have murdered Leo Caldwell. No, not murder, torture, he decided as he stepped into the elevator and punched the button for the first floor.

Only the thought of the sleeping children prevented Sunny from slamming the door. Instead, she contented herself with kicking it, then swore and hopped up and down on one foot. Limping slightly, she hurried into the kitchen. It was a mistake. She had only to look at the broken wineglass, and every word Chase had spoken to her flooded back into her mind.

He didn't want her. She pressed her fingers against her lips where his taste still lingered. Well, maybe he wanted her, but he didn't love her. And he certainly didn't need her. He'd made that crystal clear. She stepped over the broken glass and pulled a fresh one from the cupboard. Maybe he was right. She wasn't what he needed. She lifted the wine bottle, then set it back down. Still carrying the glass, she went to check on the children.

The room was lit only by the flickering images on the TV screen. Jason lay sprawled across the foot of the bed. His thumb was nowhere near his mouth. Sunny picked up a blanket from the floor and covered him. Emma had fought and lost her battle with the sandman, and the upper part of her body was propped against the headboard. Very gently Sunny eased her onto her pillow and tucked the covers under her chin. Then she turned off the TV and tiptoed out of the room.

The children were doing just fine. Maybe Chase had been right not to snap up her proposal of marriage. Absolutely right, she thought with a sigh as the wandered down the hall. After all, is this what she wanted? To be left alone with the kids? She walked into the living room. And a tipsy baby-sitter?

Sunny poured a generous amount of Alma's sherry into her glass. Everything was really for the best. So why didn't she feel happy? Or at least relieved?

And why did her heart ache so much?

She tossed back the sherry, then nearly spat it out. Coughing, she picked up the bottle and peered at the label. It was sherry all right. At least it claimed to be. She sniffed the top of the bottle. But it tasted like Aunt Alma's tea.

Setting the bottle down, Sunny strode to the couch, gripped her aunt's shoulders and gave her a hard shake. "All right, Aunt Alma. You can quit playing possum. You're as sober as I am."

Alma opened her eyes and glared at Sunny. "Stop shaking me or I'll lose my teeth."

Sunny glared right back. "Losing your teeth will be the least of your problems if you don't tell me what's going on."

Alma sniffed while she adjusted her clothes. "This was all Marnie's idea. And I have very mixed feelings about the fact that it worked. There'll be no living with her." She pointed an accusing finger at Sunny. "But she was right about one thing. It was the children that got to you. Not yellow roses."

Because she wanted to shake the older woman again, Sunny clasped her hands tightly together. "You were eavesdropping."

"The kitchen's only a short distance away. How could I help but overhear?"

Sunny sank onto the couch beside Alma and dropped her head into her hands. "I don't believe this." She drew in a deep breath and wrinkled her nose. "If there's just tea in that bottle, why do you smell like a bar at closing time?"

"I put cooking sherry in a perfume bottle and sprayed it on. What do you think?"

Sunny glared at her. "You don't want to know what I think."

"What are you making such a fuss about? It's as plain as the nose on your face that you love him. And he loves you. It's just like when Mike first met Marguerite on 'Eagle's View.'"

Sunny clamped her hands over her ears. "No soaps. I do not want to hear my life compared to a soap opera ever again."

"Well, you and Marguerite have a lot in common. It was her homing pigeon that brought Mike back to her. And Gracie's certainly been playing Cupid for you and Chase."

Sunny suddenly straightened. "Gracie!"

Alma nodded. "Exactly."

"Oh, my God." Sunny rose and started toward the door. "I forgot all about Gracie. I left her in the carriage house when I went to meet Mr. Shulman." In the doorway, she turned. "I meant to go back. But then Chase said there was an emergency here. I'll have to go." Two steps from the room, she turned again. "I can't. The children." Then it hit her. "You're sober." She whirled once more and hurried down the hall.

Alma caught up with her at the door. "You're forgetting the stakeout."

"Don't worry. I know a way to sneak in. I used to do it as a child. Hector and Chase will never know I'm there."

10

SUNNY LOCKED her car, then veered to the right side of one of the most popular picnic pavilions in Sunnydale Park. The bike path had been there for years, but it was smoother now and carried the pungent scent of freshly laid Tarvia. The clouds overhead were thick and uneven, the moonlight sporadic. But even in the dark, she had no trouble spotting the old weeping willow, its limbs brushing the ground.

Pushing her way through them, she began to climb the hill. Near the top, the incline grew steeper, and she had to grab hold of shrubs to pull herself forward. All the old familiar sensations came back to her, the tension in the muscles of her legs, the deeper breaths she had to take, the smell of moist earth and pine.

How many years had it been since she'd followed this route home from school? Fifteen? And all that seemed to be missing was her backpack straps biting into her shoulders.

At the top of the hill, Sunny paused, gauging the direction of the carriage house by the row of streetlights to her right. As the moon appeared briefly between the clouds, she glanced at her watch. Nine-thirty. It had been less than a half hour since she'd left Chase's apartment.

Still, Gracie had been alone in the carriage house for almost three hours. The thought was enough to send her hurrying down the hill. Before she'd gone far, stones shifted under her feet and she slid onto her backside. Muttering under her breath, she picked herself up and pushed the hair off her face with a shaking hand. If she broke her leg, or worse, no one would find her until morning. Grabbing handfuls of brush for support, she picked her way more carefully down the hill. Near the bottom, the shrubs became thicker and the sky darker.

Narrowing her eyes, Sunny peered into the denseness of the woods and cursed herself for having forgotten a flashlight. The first time leaves brushed against her cheek, she started and barely bit back a scream. Gradually her eyes adjusted, and she wove her way carefully through the trees until she could just make out the dark wall of the carriage house. Pausing, she listened, and at once the night sounds seemed to increase in intensity. The chorus of crickets grew louder, the whisper of wind through the leaves became a murmur, and overhead a limb groaned. Her own breathing sounded ragged, and her heart beat like the roll of a drum.

She sank into a crouch and leaned her back against a tree. Nerves, she thought. Why on earth would anyone attack her now? Squinting, she could make out the shape of the window on the wall of the carriage house. And then she heard it. A whoosh and a splash, almost like the gentle lap of waves against the shore. Keeping low, she inched her way to the window.

The clouds suddenly parted and just enough moonlight fell through to allow her to see the window was open. Even as the fear sprinted through her, she caught the scent of gasoline. Her hands trembled as she placed them on the windowsill and pulled herself onto a tree stump.

The smell grew stronger, but she couldn't see a thing. Holding her breath, Sunny got the upper part of her body through the opening and carefully reached to her right until her fingers closed around the goose-necked lamp that Hector kept next to his computer. The minute she touched it, she flipped on the switch and aimed the light slowly around the room.

A man was standing near her desk, and he dropped the upended can he was holding as he turned to face her.

"Mr. Zimmerman?" she asked. "We need to talk."

"It's too late for that," he said as he took a lighter out of his pocket and flipped on the flame. "Now please turn out the light."

"You put out that flame. My pet bird—"

"Turn off the light." He tossed the lighter into the air and caught it just as the flame sputtered out. Then with a flick of his finger, he reignited it.

Sunny snapped off the lamp. "Wait. Please. There's been a misunderstanding. You don't have to do this."

"Yes, I do."

Sunny kept her gaze fixed on the tiny flame and prayed that Hector and Chase had seen the light from the lamp. "No. Uncle Leo is willing to pay you everything he owes you."

Arnie's crack of laughter was dry, mirthless. "Don't you think I've heard that before?"

"Yes, but that was Uncle Leo talking." Sunny levered one leg and then the other over the windowsill and settled herself on the table. "This time you're hearing it from me."

"Stop," Arnie said. "I suggest you just crawl back out that window."

Sunny held her breath as the flame moved in a quick arc and then steadied. "You and I are going to talk, Mr. Zimmerman. Neither one of us is moving from this room until we do." All she could see was the tiny, dangerous curl of fire as it moved closer. All she could smell was the gasoline.

"You're wrong, Ms. Caldwell. When I drop this lighter, you'll be happy enough to crawl back out that window."

"You've never hurt anyone when you've burned a building. And you don't want to hurt me now. That's why you called this afternoon and set up that appointment. So I wouldn't be anywhere near here."

"You shouldn't have come back. I'm a dying man, and I don't have anything to lose. I need the money for my family."

Sunny could see his face now in the flickering light. And his eyes. There was pain and desperation. "You'll lose the money, Mr. Zimmerman. If you burn this building, I promise you won't get a cent." She held out her hand. "Give me the lighter and I'll give you my word I'll get the money from my uncle."

For a moment he didn't move. Then he leaned toward her and she reached at the same moment that Gracie swooped down and landed on his head. Startled, Zimmerman jumped and the lighter flew from his hand. Sunny made a grab for it. She felt it brush her fingers before it fell to the floor.

"WHERE IS SHE?" Holding up the skirt of Alma's dress in his hands, Chase paced back and forth in the upstairs bedroom of Alma and Marnie's house. Lowering his binoculars, Hector glanced up from his crouched position at the window. "Alma said she had a plan when she called. Sunny can't very well drive her car right up the driveway and walk in the front door."

"A plan!" Chase spat as he reached for the binoculars and peered out the window. "Is there a way in from the back?" The carriage house was dark, the yard quiet.

"No. The old carriage entrances were bricked up years ago."

"How about a window?" Chase asked.

Hector frowned. "There's one over my desk. But it's pretty high off the ground."

They both saw the light at the same time.

"Looks like somebody got in that way," Chase said. He was stripping off the dress even as he took the stairs two steps at a time.

By the time they reached the yard, the carriage-house windows were alight with flames. "Call the fire department!" Chase shouted as he raced across the grass.

FOR A SECOND, Sunny stared in fascination as a small ribbon of flame raced along the floor, widening as it went. Then she scrambled off the table. "The extinguisher—in the kitchen!"

Zimmerman clamped a hand on her arm and urged her toward the window. "Too late."

"My bird." Pulling away, she ran parallel to the path the fire was taking. "Gracie!" Already the smoke was billowing toward the high ceiling. Blinking back tears, she spotted the bird perched on the railing of the loft.

"I'm coming, Gracie." Hand over hand, she hauled herself up the ladder.

From below came the sound of coughing. "Hurry!" Zimmerman said before another fit of coughing overtook him.

The smoke was thicker, more pungent, in the loft. Holding her breath, Sunny set her foot on the far right side of the rung and clung with one hand as she reached for Gracie's claws. The second her fingers closed around them, she swung back onto the ladder and began her descent. Going down was slower than going up because she had to catch her balance on each rung before letting go with her hand.

Out of the corner of her eye, she could see the flames begin to lick their way greedily up the walls. On the last rung, she slipped and fell into Zimmerman, toppling with him to the floor. Rolling away, she crouched low for a moment to catch a breath of air. She'd managed to hang on to Gracie, however, and pushing herself to her feet, made it to the bird cage and shoved the bird through the open door.

Zimmerman hadn't moved. Setting the cage on the floor, she bent over him and shook him. He didn't respond. Crouched low, she tried to find air in a room increasingly filled with smoke. The flames worked furiously at the floor near her desk fueled by the gasoline. Peering through the smoke, she saw she still had a clear shot at the door. Slipping her hands underneath the man's armpits, she pulled. He didn't budge at first, but when she finally succeeded a little, Sunny fell flat on her backside. Reaching out, she grabbed the cage and dragged it along the floor until it was even with Arnie's shoulders. As she struggled to her feet, she heard a crash and a shout.

When Chase pushed through the door, he saw only flames. He heard only the roar of the fire. Then the smoke shifted and he saw her. "Sunny!" Throwing his arm in front of his face, he ran toward her. Together, they dragged the older man out onto the grass and collapsed beside him.

"Good Lord," Hector said as he raced toward them.

"Gracie." Sunny managed the word between coughs, then felt Chase's strong hands on her shoulders, pushing her back onto the lawn.

"Take care of Sunny," he said to Hector. Then rolling to his feet, he ran into the carriage house. The heat pushed him back. The smoke clogged his lungs. Dropping to his hands and knees, he coughed and then struggled to find air. When he managed to get a breath, he held it and crawled toward the spot where he'd found Sunny. His breath came out on a prayer when he knocked into the cage. He grabbed it and began to inch his way back to the door.

SUNNY COULD HEAR the sirens as she closed her eyes. Just for a moment, she promised herself. She needed to catch her breath and savor the feathery coolness of the night air, the damp chill of the grass as it seeped through her clothes. The hands on her shoulders assured her she was safe. Just one more moment.

"Here, miss. You'd better breathe in some of this."

Startled, Sunny struggled to sit up as a young paramedic slipped an oxygen mask over her nose and mouth.

"Just relax. Breathe in," he said.

Beside her, a woman was working on Arnie Zimmerman. Lifting her mask, Sunny asked, "How is he?"

"Unconscious. But he's breathing." Even as the woman spoke, she and her partner were placing Arnie onto a stretcher.

"Better check with the police first," Hector said as he let go of Sunny's shoulders and stood to walk with them to the ambulance.

"Wait." Sunny got to her feet, then her eyes widened. Somehow in the time she'd had her eyes closed, the yard had filled with people, pressing as close as the police would allow. A fire truck had pulled into the driveway, and four men in slickers were spraying a powerful stream of water onto the roof of the carriage house. She spotted her aunt Marnie with one of the neighbors by her side. Sunny took one step toward them—and then she thought of Chase. He wasn't anywhere to be seen. Suddenly she remembered. Gracie.

Her gaze whipped to the empty door of the carriage house. Smoke poured out, and flames flicked out all along the frame. Had he gone in there? Fear bubbled up into her throat, as she ran forward.

Two firemen caught her. "Keep back, miss."

"You don't understand!"

Even as she struggled, the man behind her clamped his arms around her and dragged her back several feet. Over the noise of the fire and the hose, she had to shout. "Someone's in there!"

"You're not going to join them. Don't worry, we'll tell the chief."

One fireman held her firmly as the other hurried toward the truck. Fixing her gaze on the fiery doorway, Sunny began to pray while two men donned gas masks with what seemed like maddening slowness. Then Chase crawled out, cage in hand, and they raced forward to help him onto the grass.

Once they'd gotten him to safety, Hector pried his fingers loose from the cage while a paramedic fastened an oxygen mask on his face. Sunny sank to the ground beside him and slipped her hand into his. His eyes were closed, but his pulse was steady beneath her fingers.

"Gracie's not in the cage," Hector said, glancing back at the carriage house.

Oh, Gracie, Sunny thought, her eyes filling with tears. But her gaze remained on Chase. He was safe. He was warm and alive. That was all that mattered. All that would ever matter.

THE REST OF THE NIGHT went by in a blur. When the firemen finally left, there was still the police to deal with. Sunny told her story in her aunts' living room while Alma served tea.

No one was happy with her. She could feel the waves of disapproval lapping over her when she refused to press charges against Arnie Zimmerman.

And Chase was angry with her. His silence more than anything else convinced her of his fury.

"It was an accident," she explained, and launched into the story of the night's events. When she reached the part about the lighter and Gracie, she could picture everything so clearly in her mind. She could even feel the heat of the tiny flame as it slipped through her fingers. She reached for her cup of tea, then replaced it in the saucer without tasting it.

"You refuse to charge Mr. Zimmerman, then?" the policeman asked in confirmation as he closed his notebook.

"Yes," Sunny replied.

"We're still going to question him." Rising from his chair, the other officer frowned at her. "But it's unlikely the district attorney will want to prosecute if you threaten to repeat that little story of yours on the witness stand."

When Chase followed the policemen out without speaking to her, without even looking at her, the rejection took Sunny's breath away.

A NIGHT'S SLEEP hadn't made any difference, Sunny thought as she stood on the back porch of her aunt's house and stared at the ruins of the carriage house. The air still carried the scent of charred wood. In the daylight, the damage was more apparent. The walls were still standing, but the roof at one end had caved in.

"You can rebuild it," Marnie said.

"It won't be the same."

"Nothing stays the same. Change is a part of life."

Sunny turned to give her aunt a rueful look. "I feel a story from a soap coming on. Wait. Let me guess. Someone's house burned down on 'Gallagher's Dream.'" She paused and frowned. "Actually, I think I remember seeing it a few years ago."

Marnie nodded. "Mariah Gallagher's house. They thought she was dead."

Sunny clapped her hands over her ears. "I don't want to hear this."

Marnie rolled her chair closer. "The point is that Mariah rose from the ashes like a phoenix and went back home to help her ex-husband run the hotel chain." She sighed. "That's when they got married for the second time."

"Among other things." Sunny turned back to the ruins. "Real life isn't anything like television."

"How can you say that? Last night was just as dramatic as sweeps week."

Alma called to them from behind the screened door. "You know, staring at that mess isn't going to make it go away. C'mon in. I just made some tea."

"You two go ahead. I'm going to take a closer look." Sunny walked down the steps and across the lawn. In what was left of the doorway, she stooped and picked up a handful of ashes. Slowly she let them sift through her fingers. Marnie was absolutely right. She could rebuild the carriage house. And with Hector's help and the loyalty of her clients, Service with a Smile would go on and continue to grow. On Wednesday she would play bridge at Sally Weston's and try to increase her client base.

Rising, she wiped her hands on her jeans. It hadn't been her fear of losing her dream that had kept her awake last night. It was her fear of losing Chase. He'd been very angry when he'd left. And he'd made it clear earlier in the evening that he and the children didn't need her anymore. The noise of a car pulling up the driveway made her turn.

Chase climbed out and slammed the door. Seeing Sunny standing in the charred doorway of the carriage house brought all the feelings flooding back. Frustration, anger and, most of all, fear. Why had he thought that putting a little time and distance between them would change anything?

"Dammit!" he muttered as he strode toward her, grabbed her by the arm and dragged her back to the lawn. "The firemen warned you not to go in there."

She jerked her arm free. "I wasn't going in. I was just looking."

For a moment they stared at each other in silence. He noticed the dark circles under her eyes. And the sadness in their depths. Guilt settled heavily around his heart. Still, the desire to reach out and touch her had him clenching his hands. He jammed them into his pockets.

Breathing deeply, Sunny said, "I know you're angry with me, but I am not going to prosecute Arnie Zimmerman."

"No, you're not."

"But I thought—"

"I just came from the hospital. He's going to recover from the smoke inhalation, and I wrote him a check for the full amount your uncle Leo owes him."

Openmouthed, Sunny stared at him for a second. Then she said, "Uncle Leo will pay you back."

"You can bank on it."

She nodded and then studied him. "You're still angry with me."

"No. Yes. I don't know." Taking his hands out of his pockets, Chase pushed his fingers through his hair and searched for words. "I'm more angry with myself." He began to pace. "When I picture you surrounded by those flames . . ." Whirling, he faced her again. "What were you thinking of?"

"You. I was praying that you and Hector had seen the light from the lamp and were coming to rescue me."

For the first time since he'd crashed through the door of the carriage house, Chase felt relief. Then he lifted his hands and let them fall. "Sunny, I'm sorry."

"No." She stepped toward him. "It wasn't your fault."

"I know how much this place meant to you. And Gracie . . ."

"That wasn't your fault, either!" She realized her voice had risen, but she couldn't seem to help it. "It was an accident!"

Chase began to walk back and forth across the lawn again. "I should have handled it differently. I never should have agreed to set a trap." He glanced at the charred walls. "I should have gone to the police and had them take care of it."

"Arnie Zimmerman's dying," Sunny said.

Chase stopped and stared at her.

"He wanted the money for his family. A wife and two kids. You wouldn't have wanted him to go to jail." She reached out to him then. "Whatever fault there is lies in Uncle Leo's lap."

For a moment the silence settled between them again. Swallowing the lump that had formed in her throat, Sunny said, "Well, everything's settled, then."

But when she tried to move past him, he grabbed her arm. "No, we still have the matter of your proposal to settle."

Lifting her chin, Sunny said, "I take it back."

. "Fine. Then we'll discuss the proposal I made to you." He held up his free hand to keep her from interrupting. "Let me finish. When I asked you to marry me last week, I didn't mean it." Her quick step backward had him swearing. "What I mean is that I meant it, but not for the reasons I gave you."

He ran his hand through his hair and sighed. "That makes it perfectly clear, doesn't it?" He stared at her for a moment. No woman, no man for that matter, had ever made him tongue-tied. It was time he put a stop to it. Turning, he strode to his car and yanked open the door.

Sunny's eyes widened when she saw what he pulled out. "A bird cage?" It was only as he held it up that she noticed the parakeet inside.

"His name is George," Chase said. "He doesn't speak very much yet. You'll be his first owner."

"George?" Opening the cage door, she put her hand in and gently stroked a finger over the bird's head. She felt the silver chain at the same moment the sun hit sparks off the diamond set in a gold band. Lifting it off the bird, she placed it in the center of her palm and stared at it, while hope began to blossom like a tiny flower in her heart.

After fastening the door of the cage and setting it on the ground, Chase hesitated. More than anything he wanted to gather Sunny close, lose himself in her scent, her taste. But if he did, he'd never say what he wanted to say, needed to say. Very carefully he picked up the chain and removed the ring. "There's only one reason to put it on. And that's if you love me."

She lifted her eyes to meet his, and what he saw made the knot in his stomach ease. Encouraged, he sank to one knee. "And there's only one reason I want to marry you. Because I love you. I want to spend my life with you. Not for Emma and Jase. And not for the children we'll have together. But because I want to spend forever with you."

With tears in her eyes, Sunny sank to her knees in front of him. Her hands were shaking as he slipped the ring on her finger. Then she threw her arms around him and poured all her love into the kiss. In an instant, she was weak, hot, dizzy. Would it always be like this? she wondered as they tumbled together onto the grass.

His hands were in her hair. He couldn't get enough of the texture, the scent. And his mouth never left hers as he rolled her beneath him. Then his hands were tugging her shirt free and slipping beneath it.

"Chase." There was laughter in her voice as she turned her head to avoid his lips and pushed his hands away. "We can't. My aunts . . ."

His head was spinning as he moved away. "It's nothing they haven't already seen on 'Gallagher's Dream.'"

"Probably not. But in their own backyard . . ."

Whatever else she might have said was lost as his mouth covered hers. For one final taste, he promised himself. Suddenly he felt claws sink into his scalp. "What the hell . . . ?"

"*Buenos días.*"

Slowly Chase drew away from Sunny. "Is that . . . ?"

Her eyes filled with wonder and delight, Sunny nodded and carefully coaxed Gracie off Chase's head. Then she put the bird into George's cage. "Maybe he can talk some sense into her."

"Buenos días," Gracie said. Then, *"Que sera, sera."*

"Yes," murmured Sunny as she put her arms around Chase. "What will be—"

"Is us," he interrupted. "Together. Forever."

HARLEQUIN® Temptation

Secret Fantasies

Do you have a secret fantasy?

Reporter Darien Hughes does. While celebrating her thirtieth birthday, she spots a gorgeous man across the crowded restaurant. For fun, she writes about this "secret fantasy man" in her column. But Darien gets a shock when "Sam" shows up at the paper! Enjoy #530 NIGHT GAMES by Janice Kaiser, available in March 1995.

Everybody has a secret fantasy. And you'll find them all in Temptation's exciting new yearlong miniseries, Secret Fantasies. Beginning January 1995, one book each month focuses on the hero or heroine's innermost romantic fantasies....

HARLEQUIN®

Deceit, betrayal, murder

Join Harlequin's intrepid heroines, India Leigh and Mary Hadfield, as they ferret out the truth behind the mysterious goings-on in their neighborhood. These two women are no milk-and-water misses. In fact, they thrive on

MISCHIEF & MAYHEM

Watch for their incredible adventures in this special two-book collection. Available in March, wherever Harlequin books are sold.

MOVE OVER, MELROSE PLACE!

> Apartment for rent
> One bedroom
> Bachelor Arms
> 555-1234

Come live and love in L.A. with the tenants of Bachelor Arms. Enjoy a year's worth of wonderful love stories and meet colorful neighbors you'll bump into again and again.

First, we'll introduce you to Bachelor Arms residents Josh, Tru and Garrett—three to-die-for and determined bachelor buddies—who do everything they can to avoid walking down the aisle. Bestselling author
Kate Hoffmann brings us these romantic comedies in the new continuity series from Temptation:

THE STRONG SILENT TYPE #529 (March 1995)

A HAPPILY UNMARRIED MAN #533 (April 1995)

Soon to move into Bachelor Arms are the heroes and heroines in books by our most popular authors—JoAnn Ross, Candace Schuler and Judith Arnold. You'll read a new book every month.

Don't miss the goings-on at Bachelor Arms.

HARLEQUIN®
Temptation

BA-2

On the most romantic day of the year, capture the thrill of falling in love all over again—with

Harlequin's

Bachelors

They're three sexy and *very single* men who run very special personal ads to find the women of their fantasies by Valentine's Day. These exciting, passion-filled stories are written by bestselling Harlequin authors.

Your Heart's Desire by Elise Title
Mr. Romance by Pamela Bauer
Sleepless in St. Louis by Tiffany White

Be sure not to miss Harlequin's Valentine Bachelors, available in February wherever Harlequin books are sold.

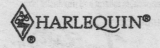

Fifty red-blooded, white-hot, true-blue hunks
from every State in the Union!

Look for MEN MADE IN AMERICA! Written by some
of our most popular authors, these stories feature some
of the strongest, sexiest men, each from a different state
in the union!

Two titles available every month at your favorite
retail outlet.

In February, look for:

THE SECURITY MAN by Dixie Browning
(North Carolina)
A CLASS ACT by Kathleen Eagle (North Dakota)

In March, look for:

TOO NEAR THE FIRE by Lindsay McKenna (Ohio)
A TIME AND A SEASON by Curtiss Ann Matlock
(Oklahoma)

You won't be able to resist MEN MADE IN AMERICA!

Bestselling Author

JoAnn Ross

Delivers a story so exciting, so thrilling, it'll have you begging for more....

Legacy of Lies

From the haute couture world of Parisian fashion to the glittering lights of Hollywood, Alexandra Lyons will find fame, fortune and love. But desire and scandal will shatter her life unless she can uncover her legacy of lies.

Look for it at your favorite retail outlet this February.

HARLEQUIN®

Don't miss these Harlequin favorites by some of our most
distinguished authors!
And now, you can receive a discount by ordering two or more titles!

HT#25577	WILD LIKE THE WIND by Janice Kaiser	$2.99	☐
HT#25589	THE RETURN OF CAINE O'HALLORAN by JoAnn Ross	$2.99	☐
HP#11626	THE SEDUCTION STAKES by Lindsay Armstrong	$2.99	☐
HP#11647	GIVE A MAN A BAD NAME by Roberta Leigh	$2.99	☐
HR#03293	THE MAN WHO CAME FOR CHRISTMAS by Bethany Campbell	$2.89	☐
HR#03308	RELATIVE VALUES by Jessica Steele	$2.89	☐
SR#70589	CANDY KISSES by Muriel Jensen	$3.50	☐
SR#70598	WEDDING INVITATION by Marisa Carroll	$3.50 U.S. ☐ $3.99 CAN. ☐
HI#22230	CACHE POOR by Margaret St. George	$2.99	☐
HAR#16515	NO ROOM AT THE INN by Linda Randall Wisdom	$3.50	☐
HAR#16520	THE ADVENTURESS by M.J. Rodgers	$3.50	☐
HS#28795	PIECES OF SKY by Marianne Willman	$3.99	☐
HS#28824	A WARRIOR'S WAY by Margaret Moore	$3.99 U.S. ☐ $4.50 CAN. ☐

(limited quantities available on certain titles)

	AMOUNT	$
DEDUCT:	**10% DISCOUNT FOR 2+ BOOKS**	$
ADD:	**POSTAGE & HANDLING**	$
	($1.00 for one book, 50¢ for each additional)	
	APPLICABLE TAXES*	$
	TOTAL PAYABLE	$
	(check or money order—please do not send cash)	

To order, complete this form and send it, along with a check or money order for the
total above, payable to Harlequin Books, to: **In the U.S.:** 3010 Walden Avenue,
P.O. Box 9047, Buffalo, NY 14269-9047; **In Canada:** P.O. Box 613, Fort Erie, Ontario,
L2A 5X3.

Name: _____

Address: _____ City: _____

State/Prov.: _____ Zip/Postal Code: _____

*New York residents remit applicable sales taxes.
Canadian residents remit applicable GST and provincial taxes.

HBACK-JM2